THE TWISTER

Julian was nursing his jaw.

'That swine hit me when I had my back turned to him,' he growled.

Mr Rex Guelder pursed his thick lips.

'There are so many swines in this city. Was it the twisting one?'

'It was The Twister all right,' snapped Julian; 'and one of these days I'll give him a twist that'll leave him permanently crooked!'

Also in Arrow by Edgar Wallace
ON THE SPOT

EDGAR WALLACE

The Twister

ARROW BOOKS

Arrow Books Limited
3 Fitzroy Square, London W1P 6JD

An imprint of the Hutchinson Publishing Group

London Melbourne Sydney Auckland
Wellington Johannesburg and agencies
throughout the world

First published 1928
New edition (reset) John Long 1966
Arrow edition 1966
Reprinted 1980
© Edgar Wallace Ltd 1966

This book is sold subject to the condition that it shall not, by way of trade or otherwise, be lent, resold, hired out, or otherwise circulated without the publisher's prior consent in any form of binding or cover other than that in which it is published and without a similar condition including this condition being imposed on the subsequent purchaser

Made and printed in Great Britain
by The Anchor Press Ltd
Tiptree, Essex

ISBN 0 09 907090 1

Introduction

By PENELOPE WALLACE

WHOEVER reads a book by Edgar Wallace has the feeling of knowing him, for he puts so much of himself into every page – his beliefs, his likes and dislikes and perhaps, above all, his sense of humour.

It was his contention that the writing of an author must be backed by experience and during his life he achieved experience in such varied fields as newsboy, printer, milkboy, medical orderly, publisher, special constable, war correspondent, journalist, racehorse owner, film director, playwright and author.

He was born in Greenwich on the 1st April, 1875. His father was an actor, his mother an actress – they were not married. When the boy was nine days old he was adopted by a Billingsgate fish porter and grew up in Greenwich and the surrounding parishes. Intelligent and observant, and having that quality of humanity which enabled him to understand as well as to observe, he acquired in his boyhood the knowledge and love of London and her people which can be felt in so many of his books.

After he left school he tried a variety of jobs ranging from printing to plastering. At eighteen he joined the army. In 1896 his regiment was transferred to South Africa. Here he wrote a poem in honour of the arrival of Rudyard Kipling, *Good Morning Mr. Kipling;* he was hailed as 'The Soldier Poet' then in 1898 a book of his poems was published under the title *The Mission that Failed.* This was the first of the 173 books which were published in the following thirty-four years.

In 1899 he bought himself out of the army and was engaged as a correspondent to cover the South African War for Reuter and later for the *Daily Mail.* By an ingenious scheme he scooped the signing of the peace treaty. The *Daily Mail* was delighted; Lord Kitchener was furious and permanently banned him as a war reporter.

With the war at an end he became the first editor of the *Rand Daily Mail* but later returned to England to the London *Daily Mail*. Here as a reporter he covered crimes, trials and hangings. He stored up knowledge of crime and criminals and he learnt two practical lessons – economy of words and the ability to meet a deadline; and later, as racing correspondent for various papers, he acquired his affection for racing which proved invaluable for his books but highly detrimental to his bank balance.

His first novel *The Four Just Men* he published himself in 1905 but his success as an author stemmed from the stories of Africa which he wrote for the *Tale Teller* and which were later published as *Sanders of the River*.

During the years that followed he wrote books, plays and articles. His success and his enormous output – in 1926 he had eighteen books published – enabled him to live in a far different way from the early days in Greenwich; he was never ashamed of his early poverty but rightly proud of his achievement.

Edgar Wallace had a remarkable memory which enabled him to work out the complete plot of a new book without making notes; invariably he wrote the first page in longhand, dictating the rest to his secretary or into a dictaphone according to the time of day – for sometimes he would work far into the night and sometimes he would begin extremely early in the morning, always fortified by half-hourly cups of tea and with a plentiful supply of cigarettes to be smoked in his long holder. His powers of concentration were immense; his young children could go to his study at any time with their problems; sleepless guests would call in for a cup of tea – but these interruptions had no effect on his chain of thought.

He worked hard and almost his only relaxation was racing and, in the summer, a journey up the river to Maidenhead in his motor launch the *Miss Penelope*.

In November, 1931, Edgar Wallace took up yet another profession; he went to Hollywood to write film scripts; he worked at his usual speed and in nine weeks he had written four scripts, including *King Kong* – this in addition to alterations to a play, short stories, articles and the long letters to his wife which were later published as *My Hollywood Diary*.

He planned that his family should join him in Hollywood before his return to England in April, 1932, but early in February he developed a sore throat; this was no ordinary sore throat for rapidly it became double pneumonia and within three days he died. He died but his books have lived; fast-moving and vital they have taken countless readers out of their ordinary lives and into the world of master criminals and little crooks; of murder and robbery. A world where right triumphs and a world which confirms that it is impossible not to be thrilled by Edgar Wallace.

The Twister, which was first published in 1928, is a typical Wallace tale of villainy, ranging from the race track to the Stock Exchange and ending vividly in the London Docks.

1

THERE was once a little trainer of racehorses and a jockey who were at variance. The third party to the dispute was a bookmaker of dubious reputation and the trouble arose over a horse called Ectis, which was favourite for the Royal Hunt Cup. Both jockey and trainer were under suspicion; they lived so near a warning-off notice that they could afford to take no risks.

This dispute was whether the horse should be scientifically left at the post, or (as the jockey suggested) whether all risks should be eliminated by a small dose of a certain drug before the race. Both men were foreseeing certain contingencies; for if the horse were left, the jockey was to blame, and if the stewards thought the animal had been 'doctored' and there was an inquiry, the trainer would most certainly depart from the turf with some violence.

Eventually, the trainer had his way. Ectis was to be caught at the gate 'flat-footed'. The bookmaker who acted for both laid the horse continuously, and from favourite he became second favourite, and from second favourite, third: from thence he drifted into the 100 to 6 class.

'I can't understand it,' said the trainer to the owner on the day before the race. 'The horse was never better, Mr. Braid.'

Mr. Braid drew thoughtfully at a long cigar, and his dark eyes fixed on the wizened little trainer. He was new to the game – in England, at any rate – an easygoing man, very rich, very amenable. He had no racing friends and knowledgeable racing men regarded curiously the slim figure with the dark, greying hair and the long sallow face and, without pitying him, expressed their regret that so profitable a mug had fallen into the hands of Lingford the trainer and his conscienceless partner, Joe Brille, the jockey.

Mr. Anthony Braid did not, apparently, pity himself. He had a small but lovely house at Ascot where he lived alone even during The Week, and he was content with his loneliness. You saw him standing aloof in various members' enclosures smoking his long cigar and looking a little vacantly into space. He seldom betted, but when he did, he betted in modest tens; he never disputed the suggestions of his trainer; he made no inquiries of his jockey. You had the impression that racing bored him.

'Possibly,' he drawled when the trainer paused, 'possibly the bookmakers fancy something else?'

'That's right, sir – they think Denford Boy is a certainty.'

Often did Mr. Lingford regret that he could not run Ectis to win – there might be a fortune for him. But he owed a lot of money to the bookmaker who was 'laying' the horse, and it meant the greater part of two thousand to lose.

An hour before the Royal Hunt Cup was run, Anthony Braid took his trainer aside.

'My horse has shortened a little in price,' he said.

Mr. Lingford had noticed the fact.

'Yes, sir – somebody has been backing him all over the country.'

He was somewhat uneasy, because that morning the bookmaker mostly concerned had accused him of double dealing.

'Yes,' said Tony Braid in his deep rich voice. '*I* have been backing him all over the country! I stand to win thirty thousand pounds.'

'Indeed, sir!' The trainer was relieved. He thought it might have been a confederate of Brille, and that the jockey was twisting him. 'Well, you'll have a good run for your money, Brille says—'

'What Brille says doesn't interest me,' said the owner, gently. 'He doesn't ride the horse – I've brought over a jockey from France. And, Mr. Lingford, I've changed my trainer. I personally handed over the horse to Mr. Sandford half an hour since, and if you go near him I'll have you before the Stewards. May I offer you a word of advice?'

The dazed trainer was incapable of reply.

'My advice,' said Anthony Braid, 'falls under two heads. One: go into the ring and back Ectis to win you enough to live on for the rest of your life, because I don't think you'll ever train another horse; two: never try to swindle a man who graduated on the Johannesburg Stock Exchange. Good morning!'

Ectis won by three lengths, and amongst the disreputable section of the racing crowd Mr. Anthony Braid acquired a new nickname. He who had been 'The Case' and 'The Mug' (the terms being synonymous) was known as 'The Twister'. And the name stuck. He had it flung at him one day in his City office, when he caught Aaron Trosky, of Trosky Limited, for considerably over fifty thousand. It is true Mr. Trosky, in the innocence of his heart, had tried to 'catch' Mr. Anthony Braid for a larger sum over a question of mining rights, but that made no difference.

'You're no better than a twister,' wailed the quavering Aaron. 'That's what they call you, and that's what you are!'

'Shut the door as you go out,' said Anthony.

Undeterred by Mr. Trosky's experience, one Felix Fenervy brought a platinum proposition to The Twister. He should have known better. Anthony examined the maps, read the engineers' vague reports (they would not have deceived a Commissioner Street office-boy) and invited Mr. Fenervy to lunch. Anthony had also a platinum proposition – a strip of territory in Northern Rhodesia. Why not, suggested the gentle Tony, combine the two properties under the title of the Consolidated Platinum Trust and take the complete profit on both flotations? The idea fired Fenervy. The next morning he paid to his victim twenty-three thousand pounds deposit and was under the impression that he was making money.

This was Anthony Braid whose wealth none but his banker knew, until that morning he came to call upon a man who closed the door in his face, a man who liked yet was irritated by him. Whether Tony Braid liked Lord Frensham or not is beside the point: his affections were, perhaps, so concentrated upon another member of the family, that Lord Frensham's suspicion and Julian Reef's hatred were matters of supreme indifference.

'Mr. Anthony Braid, my Lord,' said the butler.

Lord Frensham shifted back into his deep desk chair, ran his fingers impatiently through his thick grey hair and frowned.

'Oh!' he growled, looked at the man, and then with an impatient wave of his hand: 'All right – show him in, Charles!'

A square-shouldered man, untidily dressed, unshaven at the moment, strong-featured, big-handed, gruff of voice, abrupt of manner, this was the eighth Earl of Frensham. An obstinate and loyal man, who had gone into the City to repair a family fortune which was beyond repair, the simple, lovable qualities of his nature everlastingly fought against the remorseless requirements of his circumstances.

When Charles had gone he pulled open a drawer of his desk and took out a folder bulging with documents, opened it and turned paper after paper. But his mind was not on the affairs of the Lulanga Oil Syndicate: he was framing in his mind a definite and crushing response to the suggestion which would be made to him in a few minutes.

'Mr. Anthony Braid, m'lord.'

The man who came into the library demonstrated all that a good tailor and careful valeting could contribute towards a perfect appearance. His spare build gave the illusion of height. His black coat was carefully cut: his grey waistcoat had onyx buttons; his striped trousers bore a knife-edged crease. Mr. Anthony Braid was forty and as straight as a gun-barrel. His hair was almost black and emphasized the sallowness of the long and not unpleasant face. His eyes were dark and inscrutable. He stood, his eyes fixed upon his host, and no word was spoken until they were alone.

'Well?' challenged Frensham impatiently. 'Sit down – sit down, will you, Braid? Or are you dressed to sit?'

Mr. Braid put his hat, gloves and stick with meticulous care upon a small table, hitched his trouser-knees with great deliberation and sat down.

'A lovely morning,' he said. He had a deep sweet voice and a smile that was disarming. 'I trust you are well, Frensham – and Ursula?'

Lord Frensham was not in the mood to discuss the weather or his daughter.

'I had your letter,' he said gruffly, 'and to tell you the truth I thought it was rather an – er—'

'Impertinence,' said Mr. Braid, the ghost of a smile in his eyes.

'Exactly,' said the other jerkily. 'If not worse. What you tell me in effect is that Julian Reef, who is not only my nephew but a fellow-director, is "bearing" Lulanga Oils – in fact, that he is doing his best to ruin me. To tell you the truth, Braid, I was rather surprised that you put such a monstrous charge in writing. Naturally I shall not show your letter to Reef, otherwise—'

The dark eyes of Mr. Braid lit up.

'Why not show him the letter?' he asked gently. 'I have not the slightest fear of an action for libel. I have some six hundred thousand pounds – perhaps a little more. No jury ever awarded so much damages. There would still be sufficient to live on.'

His hearer scowled at him.

'I dare say – but that is not the kind of publicity I wish,' he said. 'I'll be frank with you, Braid. Somebody is "bearing" this stock – the prices are dropping daily – and that somebody is you! Don't interrupt, please! You have a certain reputation – a nickname—'

'The Twister,' murmured the other. 'I'm rather proud of it. It is the name that crooks give to a man who cannot be caught. And my dear friend Reef has tried to catch me in so many ways!'

'You are a racing man with a peculiar reputation—'

Again the dark-eyed man interrupted him.

'Say "unsavoury" if it pleases you. It isn't quite true, but if it makes things easier for you, my dear Frensham, say "unsavoury" – or, as an alternative, may I suggest "sinister"?'

Lord Frensham's gesture betrayed his irritation.

'It may not be true – but there it is. You are The Twister to more people than you are Tony Braid. You really can't expect me to believe that my best friend is working to ruin me – is betraying me and the board.'

The Twister smiled slowly, put his hand in his pocket and took out a gold cigarette-case, arched an inquiring eyebrow and accepted the other's nodded permission. He lit his cigarette with great care, put away the match as carefully.

'Doesn't it strike you that if I have been "bearing" your stock it is a little crude to put the blame on your friend? If I am a "twister", would I do anything so uncunning as to bring an accusation against a man you trust? Credit me at least with intelligence . . .'

The door opened suddenly and two people came in. The elegant Mr. Braid rose at the sight of the girl. The beauty of Ursula Frensham caught his breath afresh every time he saw her. She came towards him, her hand outstretched, surprise and delight in her eyes.

'Tony, you're a bad man!' she said. 'You haven't been to see us for months!'

She could not have been aware of her father's disapproving frown, though she might have guessed that the smiling young man who had followed her into the room was no longer smiling.

'I haven't come because I haven't been invited,' said Tony Braid. 'Nobody loves me, Ursula – I am an outcast on the face of the earth—'

'Don't talk like a fool,' growled Frensham.

Mr. Reef, momentarily startled by the unexpectedness of seeing the man he loathed, recovered his smile.

He smiled perpetually, this red-faced man with the thick auburn hair and wonderful white teeth. He was curiously youthful-looking despite his thirty years and had a boyish habit of blurting painful truths. Mainly they were truths that cut like the lash of a whip and not even his frank and delighted smile soothed the smart of them. Sometimes they only sounded like truth.

'Nonsense – you're getting sorry for yourself, Braid! You fellows in the fifties may keep your hair suspiciously dark and your waists suspiciously small but you can't stop yourself getting dull, old boy! I used to ask you to parties – but, lord, a wet blanket was a dry summer compared with you!'

The Twister was unruffled.

'Your parties bore me,' he said lightly, 'and when I'm bored I'm dull. I gave up your parties on my thirty-ninth birthday, which was last year. And I don't like your friends.'

Julian Reef smiled thinly.

'Don't be cats!' said Ursula reproachfully. 'Father, ask Tony to lunch today. And, Tony, behave!'

Lord Frensham was obviously uncomfortable.

'I'm not asking Braid to lunch because I'm lunching at my club,' he said. 'And, Ursula, my dear—'

He paused.

'You've got some business to talk – and, Father, you haven't shaved!'

She nodded to Tony and went out of the room. Mr. Julian Reef looked from one to the other.

'I'm in the way, I suppose?'

Tony Braid answered:

'No. This concerns you. Show him the letter I sent to you, Frensham.'

'I'll do nothing of the kind,' snapped Frensham. 'I've already told you—'

'That you do not want a scandal,' said Tony Braid quietly; 'and I assure you that there will be no scandal.'

He walked slowly to the desk and tapped the polished edge to emphasize every word he spoke.

'Until six months ago you and I were very good friends. I think I helped you in many ways – I have a larger knowledge of stock transactions than you. But I am not offering that as an argument or as a reproach. I came to your house, and you had no objection to my meeting Ursula. And then you sent me a note asking me not to call, and requesting that I should not see your daughter. This morning you have made the discovery that City sharps and racecourse adventurers call me The Twister – you have been well aware of that fact for years! You told me that I'm "bearing" your stock, selling Lulanga Oils behind your back. I anticipated that accusation by stating categorically that the man who is selling Lulanga Oil Shares, and who has brought you to the verge of ruin, is your nephew, Mr. Julian Reef, who, for some reason – and that reason can only be for his own profit – has been selling Lulangas for the last three weeks.'

Julian Reef's face was suddenly distorted with rage. He laid one hand on the other's shoulder and jerked him round.

'You're a damned liar!' he said, and the next instant was sprawling on the floor, overturning a chair in his fall.

'That will do, Braid!'

Frensham was on his feet and between the two men in a second.

'Now you can get out!'

The Twister picked up his hat, carefully smoothed the nap of it. A smile showed at the corner of his mouth.

'I owe you an apology, Frensham,' he said; 'but no man has ever called me a liar to my face and got away with it. I believe Mr. Reef is administering certain monies which are the property of your daughter. May I suggest that you send your accountants to examine that fund? It takes money to buy even yellow diamonds.'

He collected his gloves and stick at leisure. Reef, who had come to his feet holding his damaged jaw, glared death at him as he passed, but made no effort to stop him.

2

AFTER Tony Braid's departure there was a long – and to one man a painful – silence. Frensham stood by his desk, his eyes moodily surveying the blotting-pad and fiddled with a paper-knife. He was a poor man. His incursion into the City had been, in a sense, an act of desperation. There were directorships to be had. At first he had accepted every offer, but had learned by painful experience the necessity for discriminating.

Lulanga Oils was his pet; he had bought a large block of shares, mortgaging his every asset, and had refused to sell. He had faith in this stock, more faith perhaps in this clever nephew of his who had preceded him in the City by a few years.

The very success of Julian Reef, who had started almost penniless and was now accounted in certain circles as a man with a great financial future, was the shining advertisement which led the older man into the troubled waters of finance. It was on Julian's advice that he had bought Lulangas and assumed the Chairmanship of the Company. Julian it was who had suggested the administration of a fund when Ursula's aunt had died leaving her £60,000. The investments had prospered:

the gilt edge of the stocks originally purchased had deepened auriferously.

'What does he mean about yellow diamonds?'

Lord Frensham broke the silence.

'Oh, that?' Julian was his laughing self. 'The brute has discovered my hobby. I'm rather fond of diamonds, but unfortunately I can't afford to buy them, so I've trained myself into a proper appreciation of tinted stones, particularly the yellow ones which are, of course, worth only a tenth of the white diamonds.'

The other man suddenly remembered that a certain amount of sympathy was due to his nephew.

'Oh lord, no, he didn't hurt me,' said Julian lightly, though his jaw was throbbing painfully. 'He hooked me so suddenly I didn't see it coming and, of course, I couldn't retaliate – not in your house.'

'It's the last time he comes here,' said Frensham. He looked to the door and frowned warningly. Ursula came in.

'I'm sorry to interrupt – but where is Anthony?' she asked, looking round in surprise.

Lord Frensham cleared his voice.

'Anthony has gone, and he'll not put his foot in my house again. He committed a brutal and unprovoked attack on Julian . . . it's the most outrageous thing I have ever seen.'

She stared at him in amazement.

'Hit Julian? Why?'

'It was my own fault,' Julian broke in. 'I called him a liar and to him that is the unpardonable sin. I should have done the same to him.'

She was troubled, worried by the news.

'I'm sorry . . . I'm very fond of Tony. Father, are you really serious about his not coming again?'

'I'm quite serious,' said Frensham curtly.

She looked at Julian and was about to speak; but changing her mind went out of the room, Reef's sly eyes following her.

'It seems incredible,' he said, as one who is speaking aloud his thoughts.

'What?' Frensham looked up quickly. 'There's nothing incredible about a friendship like that. I should imagine he's a fascinating man with impressionable people.'

17

Julian shook his head.

'Ursula isn't an impressionable girl,' he said, and something in his tone alarmed the older man.

'You don't mean he's been making love to her, or anything of that sort?'

Julian Reef was on dangerous ground, but there was greater danger elsewhere. He preferred to play with this particular peril rather than risk the attention of his uncle straying back to another matter.

'I wouldn't say he's made love to her or that he's said anything. People don't do that sort of thing nowadays: they drift into an understanding and drift from there into marriage. I don't think you kicked him out a minute too soon.'

He took up his hat.

'Must dash to the office. My Mr. Guelder is an exacting taskmaster.'

'Where did you pick up that Dutchman?' asked Frensham.

'I knew him in Leyden twelve years ago,' said Julian patiently. Frensham's memory was not of the best, and he had asked that question at least a dozen times before. 'I was taking a chemistry course at the University and he was one of the minor professors. An extraordinarily clever fellow.'

Lord Frensham plucked at his lower lip thoughtfully.

'A chemist . . . what does he know about finance? Yes,' he said slowly, 'I remember you told me he was a chemist, and he knew nothing about finance. Why on earth do you keep him in your office in a confidential position?'

'Because he knows something about chemistry,' smiled the other; 'and when I am dealing with mining propositions and the wild-cat schemes that are always coming to me, I like to have someone who can tell me exactly the geological strata from which a piece of conglomerate is taken.'

His hand was on the door when:

'One minute, Julian: you're not in such a great hurry. Of course, I don't take the slightest notice of what that fellow said about Ursula's money, but it's all right, I suppose? I was looking at a list of the securities the other day: they seem fairly good and fairly safe properties.'

Julian's mouth was very expressive. At the moment it indicated good-natured annoyance.

'I seem to remember that Ursula had dividends at the half year,' he said. 'Of course, if you want to go into the thing as The Twister suggests – that fellow's getting terribly honest and proper in his old age – send your accountant down, my dear uncle, and let him check the securities, or turn them over to your bank —'

'Don't be a fool,' Frensham interrupted abruptly. 'Nobody has suggested that you can't handle the fund as well as any bank manager. I suppose none of the securities has been changed?'

'Naturally they've been changed,' said Julian quickly. 'When I see stock that promises to be unproductive I get rid of it and buy something more profitable. Ursula's money has given me more thought than all the other business I do in the course of a year. For example, I had the first news of that slump in Brazil, and got rid of all her Brazilian Rails before the market sagged. I saved her over a thousand pounds on that contract. And if you remember, I told you I was selling the Kloxon Industrials shares —'

'I know, I know,' said the other hastily. 'I'm not suggesting that you haven't done splendidly. Only I'm a poor man, Julian, and a reckless man; and I must think of the future where Ursula is concerned.'

Mr. Julian Reef left him on this note; and all the way to the office he was wondering what would have happened if his uncle had accepted his suggestion and had placed Ursula Frensham's money in the hands of a discriminating banker. For the sixty thousand pounds' worth of shares which he held in her name were no longer as gilt-edged as they had been.

3

URSULA FRENSHAM had a small car, and Lord Frensham's small Hampstead estate offered her an opportunity of getting away from the house without observation. She knew Tony's habits. He was a great walker. It was his practice when he called to dismiss his car and pick it up again at the park end of Avenue Road. He was half-way down Fitzjohn's Avenue when she drew into the kerb and she called him by name. He looked round with such a start that she knew she had surprised him in a moment of deepest agitation.

'Get in – brawler,' she said sternly.

'Many things I am: brawler I am not,' he said as he took his place by her side.

'Really, Tony,' she said, 'I am very, very hurt with you. Father is furious. Poor Julian!'

'I'm rather ashamed of myself,' he confessed. 'I have never quite got out of my old Barberton ways.'

'You mean barbarian,' she said. 'Tony, what is the trouble? What did you say that made everybody so angry? I know it was you who really provoked Julian. Was it about my money?'

He looked round at her in consternation.

'Did they tell you that?' he asked.

She shook her head.

'No, I guessed it,' she said quietly. 'I'm rather worried, too, Tony – not that I'm afraid for my own sake, but I think if anything happened to my money Father would die. You see, poor dear, he's been working so hard all his life and living so shabbily and the title brought none of those broad lands that a missing heir inherits, only a lot of mortgaged old country houses full of snuffy tenants. And I'm quite sure he knows nothing whatever about the City.'

'And Julian?' asked Tony, looking straight ahead.

She did not reply to this for some time.

'I'm not sure about Julian; and one really ought to be sure about the man one is going to marry.'

He opened his eyes wide at this.

'Do you mind stopping the car? I feel sick,' he said, with heavy irony. 'Whose idea is this – Julian's?'

'Father's.' She was frowning. 'Of course, it's all very much in the air. Tony, do you really think that Julian is a good financier? I don't.'

'Why?' he asked.

He thought that Julian Reef's little secret belonged to a very exclusive City circle.

'Well, for one thing, he sold some stock of mine called Bluebergs. Do you know them?'

He nodded.

'Yes, a very sound company; paying an enormous dividend. Why on earth did he sell it?'

She shook her head.

'I haven't asked. Only Sir George Crater – he's the head of the Blueberg Company.' Tony nodded. 'I met him at a dance last night and he said he was going to have a long serious talk with Father about selling the shares – he knows in some mysterious way.'

'There's nothing mysterious about share transfers, my dear,' said Tony, his eyes twinkling. He was serious again in a moment. 'Perhaps he bought something better,' he said and felt a hypocrite; for he knew Julian could find nothing better on the market than Blueberg Consolidated.

They had reached the end of Avenue Road and were turning to skirt the park when a very tall man, leaning against a lamp-post, raised a languid hand and lifted his hat with tremendous effort and almost let it fall on his head again.

'Do you want to speak to him?' asked Ursula as Tony half-turned.

'Yes, I'd rather like you to meet this gentleman,' said Tony, 'unless you have a rooted objection to hobnobbing with detective officers from Scotland Yard.'

She jerked on the brake and brought the car to a jarring standstill.

'I'd love to, Tony,' she said as she got out of the car.

The tall man was walking towards them with such a pained expression on his face that she sensed his boredom.

Tony introduced him as Inspector Elk.

So this was the great Elk! Even she had heard about this

lank, unhappy man – which was not surprising, for he had figured in half the sensational cases which forced their attention upon the newspaper reader for as long as she could remember.

'Glad to know you, Lady Ursula,' said Elk, and offered a large, limp hand. 'Aristocracy's my weakness lately. I pinched a "Sir" last week for selling furniture that he hadn't paid for.'

He looked at Tony thoughtfully.

'I haven't taken a millionaire for I don't know how long, Mr. Braid; and according to what I hear about twisters and twisting —' He surveyed a possible victim blandly. 'Education's at the bottom of all crime,' he went on to his favourite theme. 'It's stuffin' children's heads with William the Conqueror, 1066, and all that kind of junk that fills Borstal University. If people couldn't write there'd be no forgers; if they couldn't read there'd be no confidence men. Take geography; what does it do, miss? It just shows these hard-boiled murderers where they can go when they get out of the country! I never knew an educated policeman that ever lasted more than three years in the force.' He shook his head sadly. 'What's goin' to win the Stewards' Cup, Mr. Braid? Not that I hold with racin' unless I get a tip that can't lose. Racing an' betting are the first steps to the gallows. I had four pounds on a horse at Newmarket last week. It was given to me by a criminal friend of mine and it lost. The next time I catch him I'll get him ten years!'

There was a twinkle in his kindly grey eyes that belied the horrific threat.

Tony had first met the detective in Johannesburg when he went out to bring home a defaulting bankrupt. They had met since in London. Tony Braid liked this lazy man, with his everlasting railings at education; knew him for what he was, the shrewdest thief-catcher in London and though he had no occasion to ask his services, it had frequently happened that the inspector's presence at his Ascot home had enlivened many a dull evening.

'Are you looking for criminals now, Inspector?' asked Ursula, trying hard not to laugh for fear she offended him.

He shook his head.

'No criminals live in St. John's Wood, my lady. I'm looking

for my fellow-lodger. I realize I'm not doing my duty, which is to leave him to an active and intelligent police constable.'

'Has he stolen something?' asked Ursula.

'No, miss, he has stolen nothing,' said Elk, shaking his head. 'He has merely put an enemy into his mouth to steal away his brains. Which is in the Prayer Book. He's an intelligent man when he's sober, but talkative when he's soused, if you'll excuse the foreign expression. He's probably lying on the canal bank asleep, or maybe in the canal. When he's sober he talks rationally, and it's a pleasure and an education to listen to his talks about the flora and fauna of Africa; but when he's tight he talks about Lulanga Oilfields and how the wells are all dry, what he thinks of the chief engineer – well, he's a trial.'

He caught Tony's eye at that moment. The Twister was staring at him as if he had seen a ghost.

4

MR. ELK of Scotland Yard was the only detective known to fame who had ever permitted himself to be mysterious. And there was no circumstance about Mr. Elk's life that was more mysterious than the quality of lodgers who drifted to the house where he had his residence. Thieves, decayed noblemen, confidence men, and once a murderer, had slept under that interesting roof in the Gray's Inn Road. And now Tony Braid heard, dumbfounded, that a mysterious drunken somebody who knew all about Lulanga Oil Wells shared quarters with Mr. Elk. And just then Lulanga Oils was a subject which occupied his mind to the exclusion of all others.

To Ursula Frensham the topic of a possibly intoxicated authority upon Lulanga Oils was not especially fascinating. But this lank man, with the lined face and the twinkling eyes, was a figure of romance.

'He's a nice fellow, this Colburn,' Elk was drawling. 'Nothing mean about the man – a prince. Smokes cigars that a gentleman can smoke, has got a bit of money – and will get more when these shares go up.' He looked at Tony quizzically. 'I thought of seeing you about these oil shares. You gentlemen in the City could tip me off, and I'd just as soon make money out of stocks and shares as I would out of honest work. Sooner, as a matter of fact.'

'Could you bring him down to Ascot?' asked Tony, lowering his voice.

Mr. Elk scratched his neck and thought he might.

As they were walking back to the car:

'What startled you so terribly about – what's the name of the stock – Lulanga?' asked Ursula.

'Nothing very much, only I'm rather interested in the operations of that company.'

'Isn't that one of Julian's?' she asked, suddenly remembering. 'Of course: and Father has a tremendous number of shares; he's been rather worried about them.'

Mr. Braid made no reply.

She dropped him at Clarence Gate, a little mystified by his silence and very surprised when, at parting, he asked her not to speak to her father of the meeting with Elk.

He made his way to his little house in Park Street, which was both home and office, for in truth, though he had much business in the City, it was conducted from his home address, and the modest suite he rented near the Mansion House was very seldom honoured by his presence.

The moment he got into his study he picked up the telephone, called the office and gave instructions as fast as the stenographer at the other end of the wire could write them down. Within a few minutes of ringing off he had dismissed Lulanga Oils and Julian Reef from his mind, and was immersed in the study of the *Racing Calendar*.

Mr. Julian Reef would have given a great deal for The Twister's gift of detachment . . .

If you asked the average reputable man of affairs in the City of London who was the shrewdest of the younger financiers, he would have answered, a little vaguely, that he supposed it was that fellow in Drapers Gardens – what was his name again? Ah, yes, Reef – Julian Reef. There was a coterie that would have replied without reluctance, and enthusiastically, for he was very popular with a certain set.

They would have pointed with pride to his flotation of Kopje Deeps, to his daring currency deals, to that flutter in tin which nearly fluttered three old-established firms into the bankruptcy court, only they had reserves. The consequence of that flutter was that Julian, who was caught short, was within an ace of crying 'Good morning' to a registrar in bankruptcy.

There were suave and weighty men of finance who watched Julian's meteoric rise with a certain amused interest.

'He will become a millionaire, but he will never be Lord Mayor of London,' said one of these cryptically. Once Mr. Reef brought to a great house a proposition that had every promise of a cast-iron profit. The head of the house was polite, but negative.

'But, my dear Mr. Ashlein, this is gilt-edged!' protested Julian.

The wise old Jew smiled.

'It does not stop at the edge, Mr. Reef,' he said genially. 'We could not participate without being under an obligation to you and associating our house with your future enterprises. We are – um – a little conservative.'

It was the first and only time that Julian ever attempted to mix the new wine with the old: he was clever enough to realize his tactical error. It was a mistake to court the old houses – it was, he discovered, a greater error to despise the new.

Not that one would describe Mr. Anthony Braid as a financial power, new or old. He had his humble suite of offices in Lothbury and controlled a number of obscure diamond syndicates which, from Julian's point of view, were wholly unimportant. In the City he was regarded less as a financier than an authority on the sport of racing: except by those City folk who had met him in Johannesburg.

Julian came straight to his office after his unpleasant encounter with the man he hated best in the world, and Mr. Rex Guelder met him on the threshold of his private room.

Mr. Guelder was stout and shabby and spectacled. He was a native of Holland, a country which, for some curious reason, he never visited. He had a round, fat, rather stupid face, with protruding eyes and parted lips; his hair stood stiffly erect, and his careless attire was common talk in the City.

He greeted Julian familiarly and as an equal; almost pushed him into his private office and closed the door with a bang.

'Ah, my friend, I will tell you something amusing! Your ridiculous Lulangas, they fall again – three-sixteenths – a quarter . . .'

He spoke English with a certain ponderous correctness, though his speech was thick and he had a habit of rolling his r's.

'Bad luck,' said Julian ironically. 'I sold eight thousand this morning – they ought to have fallen two points.'

Mr. Guelder shrugged his shoulders and beamed.

'Does it matter – anything?' he asked. 'These things are so small, so unimportant.' He waved Lulanga Oils out of existence with a contemptuous gesture. 'The new crucible has come and will soon be put up! Also the electric furnace from Sollingen. In six weeks we shall have the new installation; and this morning the stones have come from Amsterdam!'

He opened the safe in a corner of the room, took out a wash-leather bag and carefully guiding the stones through his hand, poured out the contents on Julian's blotting-pad. Nearly a hundred cut diamonds flashed back a thousand rays in the sunlight. There were big yellow diamonds and diamonds that were so dullishly red as to be almost the colour of rubies, and diamonds of a faint, greenish tint – but never one that was white.

'What did they cost?' frowned Julian.

Mr. Guelder smiled broadly.

'Fleabitings,' he said. 'Fifteen thousand pounds. On account I have paid t'ree. Eight houses have collected them from here, there and everywhere. Their values who shall know? For us, my dear Julian, millions certain. Not because we shall sell them, as I have often told you, but because—' He tapped the side of his nose and winked.

'Put them away.' Mr. Reef was a little irritable this morning. 'Why have Lulangas fallen only a quarter? I wonder if somebody is trying to catch me short.'

Mr. Rex Guelder spread out his plump hands.

'I do not know,' he said. 'What does it matter? Why bozzer

with these oil shares, my dear Julian? You make a few thousand there, but it is playing with money, when you should reserve every centimo for the great coup!'

Julian Reef shifted impatiently in his chair.

'But is it so much of a great coup, Rex?' he asked. 'Of course, I realize that you're a deuced clever chemist and a genius at this sort of thing, but I suppose you know that we've spent fifty thousand pounds already? If anybody had told me ten years ago that I should be looking for the philosopher's stone—'

'Philosopher's stone!' snorted the other. 'Poof!' He snapped his fingers derisively. 'You disparage me. Julian you disparage my genius; you disparage science! You shall see!'

He scooped the stones carefully to the edge of the table with one hand and into the mouth of the bag, which he held open with the other; gave the leather a twist and replaced the bag in the safe. Then, quickly:

'What has happened?'

Julian was nursing his jaw.

'That swine hit me when I had my back turned to him,' he growled.

Mr. Rex Guelder pursed his thick lips.

'There are so many swines in this city. Was it the twisting one?'

'It was The Twister all right,' snapped Julian; 'and one of these days I'll give him a twist that'll leave him permanently crooked!'

He saw the slow smile dawn on the fat face of the Dutchman.

'What's the joke?' he asked.

'My friend, it is a very great joke. This morning I was talking mit – mit Jollybell – and we spoke of the twisting one. In what do you think his money is invested – what but diamonds? De Vere's, Ramier's, Orange River—'

He doubled up with silent laughter, and a new expression came into Julian Reef's eyes.

'Good Lord . . . I wonder!' he said, half to himself. 'If this thing were only sure! God! If I could catch him! And I will!'

A deeper shade came to his face, in his eyes burned the fire of a fanatic.

27

'Listen, Rex: I came to the City to make millions – not thousands. I know what it is to be poor – I am stopping short of nothing to avoid that! I don't care how I get money, or who suffers – I'm going to be rich! I'll have my villa at Cap Martin and my house in the country and my yacht in Southampton Waters. I'll have a stable of horses, though I loathe racing – I'll have a place in Park Lane and a garage of cars. And my wife shall wear the jewels of a princess. Money! It's the only damn' thing that counts. They can have everything else – I'll buy it from 'em!'

'If you are careful . . .' murmured Guelder.

'Careful! I've got to take risks. Where does all the money come from – the money we've spent on experiment? Out of trading? Careful! I'll take the gallows in my stride; but I'll have so much money that I'll make this twisting hound look like a pauper. He hit me today, Rex! Do you think I'll forget it? I'll break him – smash him. He'll be like those fellers hanging round the kerb. With a seedy old hat and a seedy old coat, shiny at the elbows. Grinning at me and asking me for a tip. And I'll spit at him!' His face had gone from red to white in the intensity of his rage and jubilant anticipation. Professor Rex Guelder, sometime of Leyden University, stared at him owlishly.

'Goot boy!' he rumbled. 'Dat's – that's the stuff. Millions, eh? Tens of millions. First the organization. Then the coup. Then all your enemies unter foot, eh? But for the moment —'

He slipped a sheet of paper toward his friend and employer.

'Sixteen t'ousand pounds, fife shillin's an' threepence – differences. You must pay today or —' He snapped his stubby fingers.

Julian was instantly sobered.

'As much as that?'

Mr. Guelder nodded.

'And we are oferdrawn mit – with der bank! Also they ask "What about it?" We must get some money – but we must keep our credit. If not, of what availing is the grand coup?'

'Sixteen thousand pounds?'

Julian looked at the other blankly. There still remained of Ursula Frensham's fortune twenty thousand pounds' worth of saleable stock. That would have to go the way of the rest.

He went to the safe and took out a long envelope.

'Sell these and put some Vaal Power Syndicate shares in their place.'

Rex went to the telephone and gave instructions. The reply had come through an hour later confirming the sale of the shares when a clerk entered the office, and behind him walked Lord Frensham.

'This is an unexpected honour,' smiled Julian.

Lord Frensham sat down heavily in the nearest chair and looked at the Dutchman, who thought this an opportune moment to make himself scarce.

Even after Guelder's departure, the visitor found a difficulty in offering his proposal.

'Julian – since you left I had a chat on the 'phone with a friend of mine.'

Julian Reef's heart almost stopped beating. He knew just what was coming.

'And, Julian – I've decided after all that those shares of Ursula's ought to be with her banker. Can I take them away with me?'

5

NOT by so much as a twitching muscle did Julian Reef betray his consternation. He looked evenly at Lord Frensham, his active mind busy. Three years before Frensham had deposited with him sixty thousand pounds' worth of safe securities. Of the original script not one single certificate remained. Bit by bit this gilt-edged stock had been sold to meet the pressing needs of the young financier, and had been replaced with script in his own companies, the majority of which was worth just the value of the securities as waste paper. Out of his own pocket had he paid, with punctilious regularity, the half-yearly dividends due on the old and sold stock.

'Do you really mean that?' he asked steadily. 'I'm rather surprised – it almost seems as though The Twister has managed to poison you with his beastly suspicions. Of course, if you want the stock back I'll apply to the bank today and send it along—'

'There isn't any question of suspicion,' Lord Frensham said uneasily. 'The point is, my dear Julian, I am making such a mess of things that I want to see with my own eyes that Ursula is secure. You'll think it childish of me, but there it is. The stock is in your bank: perhaps I could call in—?'

'I hardly think so,' said Julian coolly. 'I am not going to say anything about your attitude, Uncle John. I merely wish to point out that it would not really redound to my credit if you called at my bank with an authorization from me and withdrew the stock which is in my care. It is no secret to the bank, at any rate, that I am administering this fund on Ursula's behalf. I think you had better let me make all the arrangements for handing over this money – I mean these shares. Why have you changed your mind?'

Frensham looked past him and sat twisting his hands in his embarrassed way.

'Well, I'll be perfectly straight with you, Julian. You remember amongst the stock were seven hundred Blueberg Gold Mining Syndicate? Sir George Crater, who is the head of the Blueberg and a great friend of mine . . . well, he called me up on the phone this morning and asked me why I had got rid of these Bluebergs, he said they had risen pounds since I sold. I hadn't any idea we had sold.'

Julian smiled slowly.

'I see,' he said. 'You don't trust me.' And, when the other would have protested, he said:

'Of course I sold Bluebergs. I never made any secret of it. I bought West African Chartered that have shown a very handsome rise and a splendid dividend. It is unfortunate that Bluebergs have risen, but that was beyond my foresight.'

The older man was weakening; very shrewdly Julian pressed home his advantage.

'I don't think I've ever had such a shock as you've given me. It's knocked the bottom out of things. Obviously you have been influenced by that brute.'

Frensham shook his head.

'If by "that brute" you mean Tony Braid you can get the idea out of your mind, Julian,' interrupted Frensham quickly. 'I'm not likely to be influenced by a man whom I have forbidden to come to my house. No, it's Ursula I'm thinking of. I've got myself a bit mixed up in the City. I guess I wasn't cut out for a financier, and this slump in Lulanga Oils is rattling me.'

'They're up this morning – I suppose you know that?'

Lord Frensham nodded.

'I saw it in the evening paper – yes. But very little – they've got to jump a pound before I can get out of my trouble.'

Julian looked at him curiously.

'But what is your trouble? I think I know it all, don't I?'

Lord Frensham did not immediately reply. Watching him, Julian saw evidence of a mental struggle.

'No, I've been taking a flutter in other markets,' he said at last. 'I haven't told you, naturally, because I didn't want to feel a fool if I lost, and wanted to get a little independent kudos if I won. And I've lost. When is settling day?'

'Tomorrow,' said Julian. Too well he knew when a settlement was due!

Frensham rose and paced up and down the room, his chin on his chest, his hands clasped behind him and Julian Reef waited, but was quite unprepared for what came.

'I think I'd better tell you,' said Frensham at last. 'After my high and mighty sentiments about Ursula's money you'll think I'm the worst kind of hypocrite. But it wasn't what Tony Braid said, and it wasn't what I was told about the Bluebergs being sold – it was something else that brought me here. Some day Ursula will be a very rich woman – you didn't know that, but it is a fact: she has a reversionary interest in a very big estate. I want Ursula's present little nest-egg for myself – things have come to such a pass that I must pledge her shares against an overdraft!'

Julian's lips pursed as though he were whistling, but no sound issued.

'As bad as that?' he asked softly.

'You can't help me, I suppose?' Frensham was looking searchingly at his nephew.

Julian shook his head gently.

'You've caught me at a very awkward time. I've a deal that will eventually bring me in millions, but it's hardly likely to materialize for a few months. At the moment I'm desperately short of ready money.'

Lord Frensham continued his restless patrol.

'I know nobody who would let me have what I want . . . and Ursula wouldn't mind. I'm sure if I spoke to her she'd agree like a shot.'

'Why don't you?' asked Julian before he could trap the words.

'Because I don't want her to know I'm having such a bad time.'

He stopped suddenly in his walk and frowned.

'There is a man who would lend me money,' he said slowly, 'but, of course, I can't ask him.'

The red-faced young man did not smile.

'You're thinking of Tony Braid? The last chap in the world to help you! He's as hard as flint, that fellow; and you can bet that he'd want a *quid pro quo* that you wouldn't be very keen on paying.'

'What is that?' asked Frensham quickly.

Julian's lips twisted in a mirthless smile.

'Are you surprised to know that the aged Mr. Braid has views about Ursula?'

Lord Frensham's smile was one of amused contempt.

'You said that before. Don't talk nonsense. He isn't "aged", though he may be old enough to be her father.'

'Not exactly.' Julian was in an unusually generous mood to admit as much. 'No, he's not old enough to be her father; he's quite old enough to be her husband.'

In a long silence, Frensham walked to the window and stared down at the busy street. After a while he spoke without turning his head.

'You imagine that he's asked – oh, rubbish!' He turned round quickly. 'You see the position, Julian? I simply must have Ursula's stocks by tomorrow morning. I think we'd better arrange to send it direct to my bank.'

Julian nodded, his unwavering eyes still fixed upon the other.

'Have you no other reserves – none at all?' he asked.

He was incredulous, outraged, by the news of his uncle's penury. He almost felt as though Frensham had played him a low trick.

'I tell you I've lost and lost and lost,' said the other irritably. He passed his fingers through his untidy grey hair and stood glowering down at his nephew. An uninformed observer might have imagined that the attitude was a menace. Julian Reef knew that the big man was scowling internally at himself and his own duplicity, his own weakness, his own treachery to the daughter he loved.

'There's nothing else to be done, I suppose?' he said slowly. 'Anthony Braid is impossible. I wouldn't risk the humiliation of a refusal. No, the other way is best – the market is rising: I'll be able to unload a block of Lulangas and that will ease the situation. Send the shares to – not to the bank, no. To me at my office. As long as they get to me in the early morning that will be in time.'

With a curt nod he left the room.

Julian sat for a long time without moving, and at last put out his hand slowly and pressed a bell. Mr. Rex Guelder came perring round the edge of the door and sidled into the office.

'Something is wrong – I smelt it,' he said. 'What is the trouble?'

'He wanted Ursula's shares, that is all.'

A slow smile dawned on the Dutchman's face.

'So small a matter,' he said sarcastically. 'And how did you tell your goot uncle – nothing, of course! For if you had told him the truth he would not have gone so quietly. The adorable Ursula!' He smacked his thick lips with a grimace; and Julian did not resent his grossness but sat biting his nails, staring gloomily across the room.

'If that scheme of yours doesn't come off, Guelder, we're in the soup! Not only dear uncle Frensham and dear cousin Ursula, but a few other confiding clients may raise merry hell when they find that the shares we are supposed to be holding are non-existent. It will be a happy day for me when your new machine is working.'

'And for me,' said Guelder, rubbing his hands, a beatific smile on his face. 'Have not fear, my friend. I have had the greatest expert in the country – a German from Dresden. It is the Z-ray alone – that is the bodder. Once she is eliminated – fortune!' He snapped his fingers ecstatically. 'Greenwich shall put up a memorial to me – the greatest man of his time!'

But his friend did not share in the jubilation.

'All right,' he said; 'leave me alone, will you?'

He sat for a long time, his head in one hand, scrawling meaningless arabesques on the blotting-pad, refusing even to speak to his secretary. At five o'clock he put on his hat and went into Guelder's stuffy little office. The Dutchman was examining something under a powerful glass and looked up.

'Regard this, my friend. Is there a greater beauty?'

Julian looked curiously at the oval-shaped opal that lay on a pad of cotton-wool – a thing of fire that changed its hue with every movement of his hand: now the green of the deep sea, now a flashing orange radiance, scarlet again, blue deep and tender, and through all these colours, the shimmer of flecked gold.

Julian put down the stone.

'A mere fifteen pounds of carat,' almost pleaded Guelder. 'Such a stone is for the collector, the artist!'

'It's not for me,' said Julian harshly. 'I've got to see my uncle and tell him the truth.'

Guelder stared at him incredulously.

'Tell him . . . that the money is gone? Are you mat?'

Julian shrugged his shoulders.

'What else can I do? He'll know in the morning. I might as well get it over tonight.'

'But he will kill you, or worse, put you in prison! Do you not remember, my goot friend' – Guelder's voice was tremulous with emotion – 'what he say to you in this very room of yours? He would gaol his own brother if he robbed him! This was said with meaning – I know, I understand men!'

Julian turned on him.

'Perhaps you'll suggest some pleasant way out of it,' he snapped.

The Dutchman's face had gone pale at the hinted possibility that all his labours and researches had been in vain, and that his sublime experiment would never be continued to its logical conclusion. He was terrified. Redder and redder went his face: his neck seemed to swell. 'Better any-ting than dat! ... Raise money ... See this man Braid. He is rich.'

But Julian was not listening. Possibly his uncle, himself at the end of his tether, would understand ... he would tell him of the Great Scheme and of the millions that would come to them.

He went slowly out of the office, so preoccupied with his thoughts that he was half-way down Queen Victoria Street on foot before he realized that he had left the office at all.

Mr. Rex Guelder did not leave the office till an hour after his chief. He had the evening newspapers brought in and examined them at leisure; made certain notes in a black pocketbook which he carried in his inside pocket, and the existence of which Julian did not even suspect. At the end of his notings and his calculations he went out into the street with a smile of satisfaction on his round face, for the fates had been good to him. Though he had intended making his way homeward, he went in fact to the West End and he did not leave until two hours later.

He lived, for some extraordinary reason, as far afield as Greenwich, in a side street that runs parallel with the river. Wedged between two ancient factories, one of them derelict, was an old and dilapidated house, showing a high, blank wall, pierced grudgingly with three small windows looking out upon this mean street. The ground floor had once been a storehouse of sorts, and was now used as a garage and boathouse, fitted up by Mr. Guelder himself. Here he stored a rather ugly shaped sports car, begrimed with the mud and the dust he had accumulated in a month's travel.

Every four weeks the car was cleaned; scarcely a night passed that Mr. Guelder did not go over the engine with a loving care. This car was used for his week-end journeying to Newbury, from which he derived a peculiar interest.

It was not an ideal garage: the walls ran with moisture, and he had to keep his oil-cans locked away in a steel bin because of the big rats whose nightly squeaks he had almost ceased to notice. They came up from the river foreshore in legions some nights; he had once found the leather seat of his car in ribbons.

Then he bought his three white cats and so trained them

that every night one slept in the car: a monstrous ghost of a thing with great green eyes whose slightest squeal brought her two white brethren hurtling into the cellar.

On the floor above was his living suite: three big, gaunt rooms, plainly furnished, overlooking the river. If you opened the big window of the dining-room you looked out upon a wreck of a wharf, supported on weed-green timbers that had staggered to odd angles under the weight they no longer bore. Beneath the rotting and broken flooring of the wharf was Thames mud at low tide, and the swirling brown river at high. Opposite his window, big German cargo boats used to anchor and great tugs slept in line; and farther down, to weather-board, high-masted barges with furled brown sails and their house pennants flying made a most gallant sight for those who loved the sea and the broad commercial waters as Rex Guelder loved them.

He had a servant, a squat Dutch woman of a great age. From year's end to year's end they lived in the same house but did not speak to one another any more than was necessary. No longer even did they say 'Good morning.' Every month Mr. Guelder paid the old woman in English money, and that same day she would waddle down to the post office and despatch it all except a few pence to her grandson at Utrecht.

The sitting-room, which was also his study and library, was a long apartment running from the front to the back of the house and it was blessed with one of those grudging windows looking out on the street. The room was painted in bright orange, and all the doors, including the steel door which led to the 'factory', were scarlet. The bright carpet square in the centre of the room, the polished oak surrounds and a few Rembrandt prints on the wall gave the apartment something of gaiety. There was a blue china bowl filled with roses, and half a dozen shallow papier-mâché receptacles from which bloomed gorgeous-hued tulips. The tulips bloomed perennially, for they were artificial, but so cunningly fashioned that only those who touched them realized that the glowing petals were made of glass.

On the carpet square was a big black oak writing-table, and at this he sat. For a long time he was engrossed in the contemplation of two very common objects that he had acquired during his two hours' visit to the West End.

And as he looked at them, through a powerful reading-glass, his irregular white teeth showed in a grin of pure delight. After a while he folded them away and locked them into a dingy-looking safe that stood in one corner of the room. For a long time he mused, and then he took out a portfolio from one of the drawers, untied the tape fastening it and placed the contents where they were best inspected. They were photographs, secured with great labour by Mr. Rex Guelder and they represented something that was more than a hobby of his.

Julian Reef would have been staggered; Ursula Frensham might have believed she was taking leave of her senses if she had seen these photographs of herself, so reverently handled, so carefully placed.

He sprawled back in his plush chair, looking from one to the other, his hands clasped on the desk before him, a look of exaltation in his small, round eyes. Freda, the maid, pushed in a little dinner-wagon, saw the pictures and her old lips curled.

'There is the biggest madness of all,' she said, breaking the almost uninterrupted silence of a fortnight. 'When I see you like that, mynheer, I feel ill in the heart. Is there no such city as Amsterdam in your mind?' she asked significantly. 'And no land of Batavia?'

He did not lift his eyes from the photographs.

'They were clods, those girls, Freda. The amusement of a great scientist. Would you deny him his happiness, old vrow?'

Freda drew up a chair to the little table and sniffed.

'In Batavia they called it murder, but nobody knows who drowned her. In Amsterdam it was suicide, till the doctor spoke to the police and showed them the thin little cord about her neck.'

Mr. Guelder smiled as though he were being complimented.

'Ach! What an unpleasant memory you have, Freda!'

An impartial observer might have noticed that he was not wholly displeased, certainly unagitated by his servant's reminder. Nor had he any need to be, for no arrests were made; there had been no public scandal. The Rector of the University where he taught chemistry and electricity had merely sent for him and told him that his presence in the University would be no longer required. But then, this principal was German of origin, stout and sentimental; he had only seen how pretty, even in death, Maria was and had not realised how great a nuisance she might have been.

As to the Batavian adventure, Mr. Guelder was a little shocked that anybody should remember this against him.

The old woman was unusually loquacious tonight. He thought she had been drinking. Only when schnapps was in her did she talk so much.

'All this fooling, all these wheels and big jars and electric sparks – how will they end, Mynheer Rex? You will find nothing. You never find anything. Always you are going to. And if you did, and plenty of money came to you, it would go into the pockets of the betting men. Ach! You are foolish, and I am foolish, too!'

'You are drunk,' said Rex calmly. 'I give you food and house and money to send to your good-for-nothing student, and if it were not for me you would be starving in the streets.'

She grumbled something about his late arrival home tonight and went out. He knew that she would be silent now for a month. He liked old Freda to talk sometimes; nobody ever spoke in Dutch to him except Freda. There were hundreds and thousands of Dutchmen in London, but Rex never met them, for fear they should look at him suspiciously and talk about Maria, who was found dead in the canal with a wax cord about her throat which, as he said at the time, she might very well have put there herself.

He gathered the pictures with a tender hand, replaced them in the portfolio and locked it up. In her present mood Freda was quite capable of burning them. He finished his frugal dinner before he turned the key in the lock and passed through the red iron door into the 'factory'.

It was a long room, with a crazy, uneven floor that sloped down to one side and humped up at the end. Above, when he switched on the light, you could see the rafters and the nether side of the red tiles. There were lights enough here, for he had power to operate the many little and big machines with which the factory was equipped. The lesser of these were on a bench that ran down on the river side of the room, queer apparatus familiar enough to the electrician and the physicist; revolving wheels, green-corded coils, spiral glass tubes charged with mercury that had the appearance of enormous barometers. At the far end of the room, on a low, strongly built platform, was a machine that none would understand without examination. Here were strange condensers, coils, glass tubes which on the pressure of a button glowed rose-coloured and blue, and under one wedge-shaped pointer, connected by heavy wires to various parts of the apparatus, a square bed of black agate, in the centre of which was a tiny, saucer-shaped depression.

He pulled a chair to his bench, clicked over numerous switches and, whilst the machine buzzed and pulsated, he drew a cigarette from his pocket and lit it. Then he fixed his thick glasses more firmly to his nose and renewed for the hundredth time his great experiment. On the object he fitted into the agate depression began to flow a thin stream of crackling sparks. He touched another switch; a pale green light shot from an almost invisible slit in a steel disc, and fell athwart the agate.

He smoked and smoked till the room was foggy blue; and every now and again he would turn off his switches and, picking up the object with a pair of tweezers would examine it carefully under a powerful eyeglass. It was nearly midnight when he stretched himself and, rising, saw two green eyes surveying him from the dark end of the factory. He whistled and a great white cat came towards him to be fondled and stroked. When he got back to his room her companion was curled up in his chair.

He took a long drink of water and went to bed, and through the night the two white cats slept on the foot of his bed and opened their luminous green eyes at the faintest squeak or scurry behind the rotting panels of the room.

6

ANTHONY BRAID sat at his solitary dinner. The table was laid with the same scrupulous care as though he expected the most distinguished of visitors. He himself sat at the head of the table in a dinner jacket though he had no intention of going out. He had invited his trainer to dine with him, but the trainer had lost a train at Newmarket and had telephoned to say he would eat on the way. At half-past nine he came, an apologetic man with the lean, brown face of one who spends the greater part of his life in the open air.

'I didn't stop to change,' he said, as the maid put a chair for him. 'I bought that two-year-old, and I must say, Mr. Braid, that I'm not particularly in love with him. He's had three outings this year, and although he showed in one of them, his trainer is certain that he is a rogue.'

Braid smiled and poured him a glass of port.

'All horses are rogues if you don't understand them,' he said. 'I've only met two genuine rogue horses in my life, and I'll swear Quintil is not one of them.'

Mr. Sanford trained in Berkshire, a few miles from Newbury and after the maid had left, Sanford had a great deal to tell about his erratic charges. Anthony Braid listened intently and said very little.

'By the way, Mr. Braid, there's a new kind of tout appeared on the gallops. I don't know what to make of him. He usually turns up on Saturday and Sunday mornings. He isn't one of the regulars – I only see him at week-ends, and that's not like a real training tout. He has a house in the neighbourhood. You remember that old red building – must be a hundred and twenty years old – used to be a vicarage in prehistoric times, and then belonged to the miller. It's not much bigger than a barn . . . on the right of the road as you come up from Newbury.'

Anthony was not greatly interested in touts or old houses, but was polite enough to say that he remembered the place.

'I haven't the slightest idea what this man's doing there or what he's trying to find out – he's a German, I think.'

Anthony Braid opened his eyes.

'A German?'

'He may be; I'm not sure,' said the cautious Mr. Sanford. 'Some of the other trainers objected to him touting their horses. But I rather fancy he only comes out for a few minutes' recreation, though you never know what games these touts get up to. I remember years ago . . .'

Tony Braid listened to the interminable story of a tout who had disguised himself in some remarkable fashion and had seen a most important trial. Then:

'Why do you think he's a German?' he asked.

'His name,' said Mr. Sanford, 'sounds German to me – Max Guelder.'

Mr. Tony Braid sat upright.

'Rex Guelder, do you mean? Are you sure? What is he like – a round-faced man with glasses and a little moustache?'

Sanford nodded.

'That absolutely described him. He is a German, isn't he?'

'Dutch,' said Braid, leaning back in his chair. He was no longer bored or languid. 'Have you seen anybody else down there at his house?'

'There was only one man that ever came,' said Mr. Sanford. 'Fairly wealthy, I should think. He drives a very good car.'

'Rather young?' suggested Anthony. 'And with a red face and auburn hair?'

Sanford nodded.

'That's the chap. He doesn't come frequently; I've seen him once or twice – or rather, I've seen his car parked in the yard.'

Tony Braid was very thoughtful. He knew Rex Guelder, but only as a sort of clumsy factotum to the very shrewd and unscrupulous Mr. Julian Reef. He was not even aware that Julian was interested in such affairs as racehorse trials.

'It's probably an accident that he's there,' he said, speaking his thoughts aloud. 'I don't think that Mr. Guelder takes any great interest in racing, but I shall be able to make your mind easy on that; I have a friend calling at ten o'clock.'

He had hardly spoken the words when the front bell rang, and a few seconds later the visitor was announced.

The lank Mr. Elk had the stub of a cigar in the corner of his mouth. He loafed into the room, nodded to Tony, took a half glimpse out of the corner of his eye at the trainer before he sat down. He looked round the room at the old masters on the wall, at the priceless tapestries, and his lips curled in a sneer.

'My idea of a slum,' he said.

Tony pushed the cigar box towards him and he selected a Corona with great care.

'Cigars are my weakness,' he said; 'picked up the habit in America. I'd have let Crippen go for a couple of boxes of good Odoras.'

He bit off the end, lit the weed and drew luxuriously.

'I'm all for corruption and bribery,' he said. 'What's in that decanter, Mr. Braid? Looks like red ink . . . port, is it?'

He helped himself.

'Drinking and smoking are the ruin of the lower middle class – and betting,' he added. 'They tell me your horse Barley Tor is going to win the Stewards' Cup. I doubt it.'

'Mr. Sanford will be able to tell you something about that,' said Tony.

Elk nodded.

'I knew it was Mr. Sanford – saw his picture in the paper the other day – a very classy paper. Full of pictures of people making faces at race meetings: Lord This and Lady That, the Honourable Mrs. Somebody with the Honourable Mr. Somebody Else. That's what I call class. Not that Barley Tor will win any Stewards' Cup' – he was going off at a tangent when Tony interrupted him.

'You know most of the racing crowd, don't you, Elk?'

Elk nodded.

'Do you know a man named Rex Guelder – a Dutchman?'

To his amazement Elk nodded again.

'Systematic Samuel. Yes, I know the man that works his commissions. There's no mug like a foreign mug.'

'But surely you're mistaken?' objected Braid. 'The man I'm thinking of is—'

'Assistant Managing Director to Julian Reef, Esquire, millionaire and getabit,' said Elk; 'and I'm never mistaken, Mr. Braid. It's practically impossible for me to go wrong. I happen to know because one of the bookmaking classes who calls himself a friend of mine, Isadore Wayne, asked me if I

42

knew this poor Hollander who was on the back of his book for three thousand pounds. And Wayne is a long-suffering man who never bleats.'

Trainer and owner exchanged glances.

'I'll tell you something else. It was Guelder who accidentally put me on the track of this stumer of yours, Barley Tor. He's backed him with Wayne.'

'Then he *is* touting,' broke in Sanford. 'He was on the ground when I gave Barley Tor a rough gallop the other day.'

'Why do you call him Systematic Samuel?' asked Braid.

Mr. Elk sighed.

'If there's one thing I hate more than another it's giving long explanations, Mr. Braid,' he said. 'But that's what old Wayne calls him. He backs horses on a system. It appears this man Guelder is on the scientific side. He was a professor or something, but got into a mess a few years ago and left Amsterdam in a hurry – or maybe it was Rotterdam. I know there was a "dam" in it. We got no inquiries from the Dutch police, so I suppose the girl wasn't popular. She was a friend of his, and died suddenly. Drowned. Some said it was suicide – but not many. Anyway, Guelder's clever. They say he spends his time looking for the – what is the word – of life?'

'The elixir of life?' smiled Tony.

'That's the word, "'E likes her." I don't know what it means, but it sounds fine. And then he got a crazy idea that he could discover something or other that turns lead into gold. There are quite a lot in Dartmoor who have made the same discovery and got time for it.'

This was information indeed to Tony Braid. He knew Guelder by sight, had spoken to him once or twice and never once had the gaunt-faced Dutchman made the slightest references to horses. Tony said as much, and Mr. Elk smiled pityingly.

'No man goes round boasting of his vices,' he said, 'except golfers. This feller Guelder is the world's mug punter. He's lost thousands.'

Tony was a little troubled. He did not love Julian Reef, but he was satisfied in his mind that the red-faced young man had no knowledge whatever of his friend's peculiar weakness; from his own knowledge, neither Guelder nor Reef could afford to lose thousands a week; and if this leakage was going on in the business, somebody was getting hurt. He was well enough acquainted with Julian to know that in spite of his seeming prosperity, he lived dangerously close to crisis; and a crisis in Julian's affairs might very well hurt Frensham – and Ursula.

The news was disturbing for that reason. He did not doubt Elk for one second. This lean detective was a mine of information on the most unlikely subjects. His failure to pass qualifying examinations had compelled him for years to occupy a position which gave him, perhaps, a greater opportunity for gaining knowledge of men and things than he might have had if he had procured his promotion, and had been relegated to some cut-and-dried office. He collected facts about men and women with the assiduity and fanatical eagerness that others devote to the collection of stamps. And his memory was prodigious. He might not, as he had often said, recall the exact date on which Queen Elizabeth reviewed her army at Tilbury, but he knew just where Johnny the Lag got that long scar at the back of his head, and why a certain member of the Government had died with such extraordinary suddenness. Many of the closely guarded secrets which their owners fondly believed were tucked away in the black deed-boxes which adorned their lawyers' offices were so familiar to him that he had almost forgotten them. Almost – but never quite; for he could draw from the back recesses of his mind, at any given moment of need, the most appalling and damning details of stale romances, dead follies and half-obliterated acts of crookedness.

'Do you know Lord Frensham?' asked Tony.

Elk nodded.

'Friend of yours, ain't he? Good feller, but broke. I was in St. James's Street the other day, making inquiries about a common felony, and I had a look at his office. I'll bet you didn't know he had an office in St. James's Street.'

Tony smiled broadly.

'That's one of the things that I do know,' he said. 'Lord Frensham has a number of business interests which he operates from there.'

Elk was not abashed.

'Thought you might. But I'll bet you don't know the history of the flat he's got – at least, it used to be a flat.'

Before Tony could ask a question the door opened and the maid appeared. Braid had heard the telephone and was already half-way to his feet. He knew that the call was an important one, for the girl had orders not to disturb him otherwise.

'Miss Frensham, sir.'

Braid went quickly into his study and took up the receiver.

'Is that you, Tony?' Ursula's voice was tense, a little terrified, he thought, and his heart sank. 'Can you come up, please? My father has not been home to dinner! I think something rather dreadful has happened.'

'I'll be up in five minutes,' he said. 'Don't worry. It isn't very late, is it?'

'N-no, only he asked me especially to stay in for him. He wanted me to find something.'

Tony Braid came back to his guests, excused himself to Sanford, and a few minutes later he and Elk were driving towards Hampstead.

'What's the trouble with Frensham?' asked Elk.

'Nothing very much,' said Tony evasively.

'Queer that young lady should worry about his not coming home.'

A little later:

'I may as well tell you, Elk: you've been a very good friend of mine, and I've proved that you can be discreet. Frensham is in pretty bad trouble. Just before dinner tonight he telephoned me and asked me if I could lend him seventy-five thousand pounds.'

Elk whistled.

'And naturally you said no,' he said. 'I'm all for it! If I had the money paid back to me that I've lent, I'd be a rich man.'

'Of course I said yes,' said Tony quietly. 'In fact I sent the cheque by special messenger to his office.'

'Then why not go to his office first?' asked Elk.

Tony shook his head.

'I called him up an hour after I sent the money to ask if it was enough, and there was no answer.'

'Was the cheque delivered?'

Elk was curiously interested.

'Yes; I checked up, it was given to Frensham.'

Elk asked no further questions, and presently they came to the house and found Ursula waiting for them half-way down the short drive. Tony stopped the car and jumped out. Mr. Elk, in his evasive way, faded into the background.

As Tony drew the girl's arm in his he could feel her trembling.

'What are you worried about? Why are you so scared, my dear?' he said, patting her hand. 'It is I who ought to be worried – your father told me I was not to put my nose inside his demesne, and here am I holding his daughter's hand in the most shameless way.'

'Tony,' she said in a low voice, 'Julian is here. He came a quarter of an hour ago. He said he went to Father's office but could get no answer.'

'Julian here?' said Anthony in dismay. 'That's rather awkward: I shall have to do one of my famous twists and be nice to him!'

Any doubt he might have had as to Julian's attitude was removed the moment he came into the house. The red-faced young man was pacing up and down the broad hall and came towards him with a nervous smile.

'I owe you an apology, Braid,' he said. 'I bear you no ill will for that left hook of yours.' And then he went on quickly in a more serious tone: 'I'm worried about Frensham. He was at my office this afternoon and we had a heart-to-heart talk about shares. He wanted me to hand over to him a block that I was holding for Ursula. In point of fact, he has had those shares in his possession for the past three months. He was so extraordinarily strange in his manner that I thought he was ill. I should have rung up Ursula, but I didn't want to alarm her.'

They were in the drawing-room now; it was a hot night, and Tony gathered that the french windows were open by the swaying of the curtains which were drawn before them.

'I called at his office tonight,' Julian went on, 'but there was no answer so I came on here.'

'Does he usually work so late at his office?' asked Tony.

'Very often.' It was Ursula who spoke. 'He has been there night after night lately – I think he's been worrying about the Lulanga Company. I shouldn't have been worried about him being late but he's always so punctual for appointments, and he did ask me to be here at half-past eight. I put off a theatre partly because he said it was important.'

Tony was scratching his chin thoughtfully, his eyes still on Julian Reef's face.

'I will go down to St. James's Street and see what is delaying him,' he said slowly.

'If you like I'll go with you,' volunteered Julian.

But Tony shook his head.

'It isn't necessary; I have a friend in the grounds somewhere – Inspector Elk: you may have heard of him.'

'Elk?'

Even Ursula was surprised at the change in the man's tone; it became suddenly harsh and hard. He almost shouted the word.

'Elk? That long fellow . . . oh yes. I know him. Is he here? How odd!'

His face had gone from red to white, from white to red again.

'Yes, I've met him. A queer Scotland Yard bird who's always talking about education. Then you won't want me.'

When Anthony got out into the drive he found Elk leaning against the car, a cigar between his teeth.

'Miss Frensham is rather worried about her father's absence. I'm going down to his office.'

'I know,' said Elk as he got into the car. 'That Reef fellow was awfully cut up about me, but when he says I talk about nothing but education he lies in his boots!'

'How do you know what he was talking about?' asked the astonished Tony.

'I was listening at the window,' said Mr. Elk calmly. 'I find that's one of the best ways of collecting information – listening and saying nothing. What's that about the shares and the cheque? Big fellow, that man Reef – thinks in millions, talks in tens of thousands and pays in ha'pennies.'

When they got to the building where Frensham had his office they found the outer door closed; and Anthony would have gone back to Hampstead but for the detective's insistence on making another attempt to get in.

'There's a caretaker in this building and a couple of office cleaners – I know to my certain knowledge. Give a bang on the door, Braid.'

Tony carried out instructions, and after a while was rewarded. A charwoman opened the door a few inches and, when Mr. Elk revealed himself and his profession, admitted him in a fluster.

'No, sir, we haven't been in Lord Frensham's office,' she said. 'It's a very peculiar thing: we've got all the pass-keys, but they won't open his door. My friend says that it must be bolted on the inside.'

They went to the second floor and the woman showed him, with the help of the pass-key, that the door was immovable. It was a typical office door; the upper half was of opaque glass inscribed 'Lulanga Oil Company, Limited'.

'In the circumstances,' said Mr. Elk, 'all things are justifiable – lend me your broom, mother.'

The woman handed him a short hand-brush and on his instructions stood back out of reach of flying glass. Two taps shattered the pane, and Mr. Elk very cautiously removed a jagged piece of glass before he put through his hand and drew back the bolt. Then he handed back the brush with a bland smile.

'Now you can go downstairs. If we want you we'll send for you,' he said, and reluctantly the woman, scenting mystery, descended to the lower floor.

'I hope your stomach's strong,' said Elk, for he had seen ...

A click, and the light flashed on. Frensham was sprawling over a writing-table, his head upon his hands; the white blotting-paper was speckled red, and in the clenched white hand that lay on the desk was a revolver.

7

IT was Elk's matter-of-fact voice that brought Tony Braid to his senses.

'There's a 'phone over there. Just ask for the police-station; tell them there's a death here and that you want the divisional surgeon.'

'Dead?' whispered Tony. 'Good God!'

Elk looked at the stricken figure with a thoughtful eye, and then he saw the paper. It was not on the pad, but a little to the side.

The detective took it up and read a few lines with a frown.

'Do you know that handwriting?'

Tony nodded. It was Frensham's beyond any doubt. His mind in a whirl, he read the fateful message:

For years I have been engaged in foolish speculations. I confess that I have taken monies which are not mine, particulars of which are set forth below. I am not fit to live . . .

Here the writing ended abruptly.

'Is that Frensham's writing?' asked Elk again.

'Undoubtedly,' said Tony in a hushed voice, staring fascinated at the still figure.

Death he had seen in many shapes; tragedy in its most hideous aspects; but there was something awful in this sprawling body and all that it stood for.

Whilst Tony telephoned, the detective walked to the window, pushed it up and, leaning out, sent his torch flashing on either side. He pulled the window down again and fastened the catch.

By the side of the desk was a waste-basket the bottom covered with torn paper. This he shook out on to the small table where the telephone stood, and sorted over the contents.

'I guess he got your letter and cheque all right,' he said after a while.

He pointed to a little heap of paper which he had separated from the rest.

'Here's the cheque, torn into bits – at least, I suppose it's yours.'

Before Anthony could piece together the fragments of the pink slips, he knew it was the identical cheque he had sent.

'We'll keep these.' Elk took an envelope from the stationery rack on the table and put the little fragments carefully inside. 'And the letter and envelope, too. It looks as if it was torn up unopened.'

The district surgeon arrived a quarter of an hour later and made a brief examination. Frensham had died instantly.

'Now I think you've got the dirtiest bit of work to do,' said Elk.

Tony nodded and went slowly down the stairs to Hampstead to break the news to Ursula.

He found her waiting for him at the open door of the house, and one glance at her face told him that by some means she already knew, and that the most tragic part of his task had been anticipated.

'Come in, Tony.' She was very white, but her voice was wonderfully steady. 'Mr. Elk has been on the 'phone – he didn't tell me everything, but I think I can guess. Is he dead?'

Tony nodded.

'How dreadful!' She put her hands before her eyes and shuddered. 'Does Julian know?'

'Isn't he here?' asked Tony in surprise.

She shook her head.

'No; he left just before Mr. Elk telephoned. I told him how good you had been to Father . . . I mean, about the money you sent him tonight.'

Anthony stared at her open-mouthed.

'How did you know that I sent him money?'

She did not answer until they were in the panelled dining-room and had closed the door.

'Father told me he was in trouble and that he'd asked you to help him. He told me over the 'phone earlier in the evening.'

'But you didn't know—'

'I knew you, Tony,' she said quietly. 'If he asked you for money I knew you would have sent it. He wasn't so sure you would, poor darling! He told me to be here at half-past eight in case you hadn't, but that he'd be back in any case by then.'

She was very quiet, very brave.

He did not wish to distress her by discussing money matters that night, and he was somewhat surprised when she herself broached the subject.

'Do you think my money has gone?' she asked, very calmly. 'I never discussed it with Father,' she went on. 'He was rather difficult and touchy. My dividends used to come in every half-year, and I have quite a respectable amount in the bank.'

'How long has he handled your estate?' asked Tony.

She shook her head.

'I don't know. It was news to me, and rather surprising, that Julian had handed over my shares at all.' She shook her head. 'I wonder if you think I'm heartless to discuss this now,' she asked. 'Do you realize, Tony, that you have rather a heavy responsibility?'

He looked at her without understanding.

'What is it?' he asked.

'You were the trustee of Father's estate. He never altered the will he made years ago. He spoke about it when he was so angry with you this morning and said he was going to make a different arrangement. I think he intended putting Julian in your place. Tony, you dislike Julian, don't you?'

'I'm not very fond of him, but at this particular moment I'm not making things any harder by perpetuating my own dislikes,' he said.

'I don't dislike him,' she said; 'he's terribly masterful in his way; and his partner, or whatever he is, is a horror.'

'Guelder?' asked Tony quickly.

She nodded.

'I had no idea you knew him.'

She was silent, and he did not press her. This was a new and remarkable discovery. He felt there was something behind that chance reference to Julian Reef's confidant, a hint of fear that only his sensitive mind could register.

It was half-past two in the morning when Elk came to Tony Braid's house. He found his host wearing a silk dressing-gown, a fact upon which he immediately commented.

'Pity you're undressed; I was going to ask you as a personal favour to step along to St. James's Street and have a look round. How's the young lady?'

'I've persuaded her to stay with some friends of hers in Hampstead tonight,' said Tony, and Elk nodded long and slowly. 'As to going to St. James's Street, I shall be almost grateful for the occupation – I am not likely to sleep tonight.'

He was dressed under the gown save for his jacket and shoes and, while he put these on, Elk told him the latest news.

'I've been interviewing that messenger-boy who delivered the cheque. It sounds a funny business. He got to the office about a quarter to eight and the door was locked. Frensham didn't open it, but asked who was there and told him to push the letter under the door. I've got the boy's receipt in my pocket – just an "F", that doesn't tell us anything.'

'What excuse did Frensham give?'

'Said he was changing,' said Elk. 'He did change sometimes: I found a small wardrobe in the inner office. Queer he should have torn up that envelope without opening it,' he said. 'Did he know your handwriting?'

'It was typewritten,' said Tony. 'I had a number of envelopes addressed to Frensham – we conducted quite a correspondence in the old days.'

'Humph!' said Elk thoughtfully. 'Maybe he thought it was another bill. There were scores in the desk. Frensham's in a pretty bad way financially.'

Tony announced that he was ready, but Elk did not rise from his chair.

'I used to know that flat before it was an office,' he said. 'There were more burglars there than in any other flat in London.'

Tony thought he was being merely reminiscent and yet he should have known his man well enough to be sure that his words had some special application.

Elk rose suddenly and intimated he was ready, and they left the house together and got into the waiting police car. There was a policeman on duty at the door of the building in which the office was situated.

'A clever idea,' said Elk, bitterly, as they climbed the stairs to the second floor. 'He might as well be stationed at the bottom of a tube!'

He unlocked the door with the shattered panel and ushered Tony into the death-room. There was little evidence of the tragedy which had occurred. Frensham's body had been removed, even the bloodstained blotting-pad had been taken away, though there were still sinister stains upon the writing-table.

'I thought,' began Elk, 'we might take a look—'

He stopped suddenly, and Tony saw him staring at the window. A pane of glass had been broken there too, and glittering splinters lay on the carpet beneath the window. Mr. Elk did not say very much, but for a second he looked rather unhappy.

'Glass broken, catch turned – and I told that damned – that feller to keep a man outside the door; this door!'

'What's happened?' asked Tony.

'Somebody's been in the room, that's all. Came in from the outside. Couldn't have been a reporter – reporters only do that sort of thing in books.'

He pulled up the window and leaned out, and then, to Tony's alarm, threw one leg over the sill and disappeared from view. For a second Anthony Braid thought the officer had gone mad, but a cheery voice near at hand reassured him, as he looked fearfully out into the darkness.

'It's all right,' said Elk. 'This is the way the burglars used to come. It was like eating jam.'

He was standing on a narrow iron balcony which ran immediately beneath the window and extended, Tony discovered, to a circular staircase.

'A fire-escape,' explained Mr. Elk. 'You can either call it that or the burglar's joy-plank. Give us a hand.' Tony gripped the other powerfully and drew him up through the window.

'Do you mean that somebody broke in here tonight after the body was moved? Why?'

Elk shook his head.

'To take something – maybe one of them – those secret documents you see in plays. You never know. Or the family jools. Or the letter showin' who's the rightful heir.'

'But seriously?'

Elk could give no information.

'If I could tell you why, I could tell you a lot of things that nobody knows – as yet!'

He began a systematic search of the 'office'. It had been, as he said a small flat; contained three fair-sized rooms, two of which were evidently used by a fairly large clerical staff.

'What I can't understand about you,' said Elk as they left the building after completing their examination, 'is your uncuriosity! You haven't asked me once how Frensham shot himself.'

'I never ask unnecessary questions,' said Tony.

8

THERE were two dreary days of police inquiry and the uncomfortable inquest; and if Tony Braid was averse from asking unnecessary questions, there were a couple of stolid jurymen who did not share his objection. The proceedings dragged themselves through four columns of print to an inevitable conclusion, and the jury returned a verdict of 'Suicide whilst of Unsound Mind.'

Happily, it had not been necessary to call Ursula, and on the afternoon of the inquest she left for the country. She took a farewell of Tony over the telephone, declined his offer to drive her to Somerset and would have gladly dispensed with the visit which Julian Reef paid to her a few minutes before her departure.

She had two letters from him, long, intense epistles which she had not even read through. He had made several attempts to see her, but she had found an excuse for refusing an interview.

Why she was behaving like this to him she herself did not know. Only – she hated even to admit this – almost with the pang it brought, the news of her father's death had given her the faintest sense of relief. She analysed it down to a first cause in her ruthless way. She would never have married Julian in any circumstances, but the unconscious and imperceptible pressure which her father's wishes had brought to bear on her would no longer be exercised. She was mistress of herself, ruined, she guessed, except for a small income which came from her little property near Morpeth, but none the less free.

She had been fond of her father, and his sudden death had been a stunning shock to her; but if the truth be told, her relationship had never been of that intimate, cordial character which she might have felt had Lord Frensham been less preoccupied in his rainbow of chasing wealth.

She was actually pulling on her gloves and taking a last look round when the maid announced Julian. It was too late to find excuses; Mr. Reef walked in immediately on the girl's heels. He was soberly dressed; his black tie and the deep black band about his hat she thought was a little archaic, and for certain reasons unnecessary.

'I've been trying to get you ever since this horrible affair—' he began.

'You've got me now for five minutes, Julian,' she said.

Her coolness was a little unnerving to him. She was rather different from the willing girl he expected to find.

'Well . . . your position – and everything,' he began, lamely. 'I don't know what your father has left, but I can guess his affairs are terribly muddled. Naturally I can't allow you to want for anything. I suppose this house will be sold—'

'I don't know why,' she interrupted. 'The house belongs to me – didn't you know that?'

He was taken aback, irritated by her self-possession.

'You don't seem to be very upset by your poor father's death – not as much as I should have expected,' he blurted out. 'Of course, it's no business of mine, but you've got to remember all that Frensham did for you when you were a kid—'

'I certainly don't need you to remind me of it, Julian. I am overwhelmed by this awful thing. But you don't expect me to wear black, or mope – Father would be the last to wish that.'

There was an awkward silence here; all his well-remembered speeches failed to march with opportunity.

'I suppose things are in a muddle,' he went over on a new tack. 'They tell me in the City that Braid is administrator of the estate. That is an outrage, when you consider what your father thought of him. I'm perfectly sure, if your father had realized that he had appointed this rogue as executor and trustee, he would have made some change before he committed this . . . ghastly act. Lord Frensham loathed him.'

She was looking at him thoughtfully, biting her lip. Now she shook her head.

'Could he loathe him if he asked him to lend him money at the very last moment?' she demanded quietly. 'That doesn't sound as though there was any very bitter enmity, Julian. And I wish you would remember that Tony is a very dear friend of mine.'

'So I understand.' His full lips curled in a meaning smile, but she ignored the implied insult.

'He didn't succeed in helping Father, but at least he showed willingness. He has been more than kind to me – and to you.'

He frowned at this.

'I don't know what you mean, Ursula. How has Braid been kind to me? I haven't noticed it.'

'I will tell you,' she said slowly. 'It was he who suggested that we should not inquire too closely into the question of the sixty thousand pounds you held on my behalf—'

'Your father had it,' suggested Julian loudly, his face suddenly going a deeper red.

She ignored the interruption.

'Tony suggested, and I agreed, that we shouldn't inquire too closely as to where that stock was held and to whom it was transferred and when. It is rather easy to trace shares, Julian, isn't it? I know nothing about the City and the stock market, but I'm sure that Tony could have discovered what happened to my shares, and when they were transferred to Father.'

'I can show you the transfers—' he began, and stopped. He was enraged at the sight of her contemptuous amusement. 'Really, Ursula! Remembering that you will one day be my wife, your attitude is extraordinary!'

It was a bold stroke on his part: he was putting all he had at stake to this one test. That he had failed, he knew before she spoke.

'I don't think that is a matter even for future discussion,' she said quietly.

The interview was going in the very worst way for him. He had come to learn, under cover of his sympathy, the truth about this legacy which was due to her. Frensham had said she would be a very rich woman – it was the first he had heard of such a possibility, and he was consumed with curiosity to discover how much there was in the dead man's word. And he found himself on the defence, confronted with what was to him a staggering half-accusation. For there could be no doubt what Ursula Frensham meant, when she said that neither she nor Tony Braid would inquire too closely into the fate of her stocks.

He was staggered and a little frightened; half his secret seemed public property when she spoke; he had a moment of panic when it required every effort of will to prevent himself flying from her presence.

'I don't know . . . it seems very extraordinary . . . ' He was incoherent, embarrassed beyond immediate recovery. 'You've evidently been listening to lies. The Twister! Good God! You won't take any notice of what he says, surely? After all these years . . .'

Ursula knew that this was the moment to dismiss him. There was really nothing quite so sickening as to see a man she had trusted, and in whose integrity she had had the greatest faith, in the position of a suppliant. For he was pleading now, not knowing for what he pleaded, consumed with a shaking fear that she might know more, much more, than she had told him, and shocked that she knew so much.

'For God's sake, Ursula, be reasonable! I realize what a terrible blow this has been to you . . . Your father's death and everything . . . Don't believe these ugly things of your friends. You know Braid's reputation is foul! He has lived on lies, built up his fortune by trickery . . .'

So far he got when she opened the door for him. He tried to think of something definitely crushing, but for the moment his brain was numbed. She watched him disappear down the drive, and heaved a deep sigh. It was the first moment of satisfaction she had had since that dreadful night when Elk telephoned the news of her father's death.

The moment she reached Somerset she wrote Tony a long letter:

I'm going to be completely heartless and forget and forget and forget. If I let my mind dwell on this horror I think I should go mad . . . I had a great respect for Father, and I suppose I am being heartless when I thank God that he always kept himself and his thoughts so far distant from me that he never gave me a chance of loving him. I hope you will go to your racing and not worry about me . . . The butler here is most anxious to know if Barley Tor is what he calls 'the goods'. Am I to tell him yes? I have never asked you for a tip before: you must give me one now.

Tony was at Ascot, a very busy man. He had resolutely refused the invitation of Frensham's lawyer to go through his late client's papers, and had written saying that he would not take up his duties seriously till the air of Berkshire had blown away a few gloomy memories.

Braid was something more than a complacent owner. He knew horses as well as he knew men. To him the significance of a gallop was as plain as though it had been written down by the horse himself.

He drove early one morning to Newbury to see the winding-up work of his horses, and after breakfast he rode out with his trainer to the gallops.

'There's the house I was speaking about – the Dutchman's house,' said Sanford, pointing with his hunting-crop to a rambling old red building that stood back from the road. It had a neglected appearance; the garden was a mass of weeds, and two grimy window-panes on the upper storey were broken.

'He was down here on Saturday, as usual, and there is no doubt of his being a tout. My head lad tells me that he has been haunting the village inn, picking up any information he can get about Barley Tor.' He laughed softly.

'Is he here now?' asked Tony.

'That's what I was going to say. Usually he doesn't come till Friday night or Saturday, but he turned up last night and I expect we shall see him at the end of the gallops. That's rather a nuisance, because you wanted these horses tried this morning.'

'Not at all. It isn't a nuisance,' said Tony. 'I couldn't wish for anything better.'

'Of course we can run the wrong way of the trial ground and finish the other end of the gallop,' suggested Sanford, but Tony shook his head.

'A twister I am, and a twister I will remain till the end of the chapter!' he said. 'Let me justify my title. If Mr. Rex Guelder is anxious to know the chance of my horse in the Stewards' Cup I am going to give him the twist of his life.'

'There he is,' interrupted Sanford, suddenly.

9

THEY were passing along the white road that runs across the downs. The ground slopes up from the road, and on the crest stood the incongruous figure of Mr. Rex Guelder. Incongruous because of his straw hat, black coat and bright brown shoes. Under his arm was a folded umbrella; his hands were encased in bright yellow gloves; and dropping from his large, ugly mouth was one of those thin cigarettes of a size usually devoted to the use of ladies.

As Tony put his horse to the slope, he turned and raised his hat with a flourish.

'Guelder!' he barked, introducing himself with a stiff little bow, in the German way. 'I have the goot pleasure to see Mr. Braid? We have met, I think, in the more serious business of finance.'

Tony's eyes twinkled.

'I had no notion that you were interested in the flippant business of racing,' he said.

'A leetle,' said Guelder quickly, 'only a very leetle. I come to see the beautiful horses, to forget all my troubles in the City. Here I stand, with the wind of the good Gott in my face, and rejoice to be alife!'

Tony looked down into the round and brutish face on which the winds of the good Gott misguidedly played, and for the first time in his life seriously made a study of the man who had so piqued his curiosity. Elk had told him some curious stories about Rex Guelder; and there was confirmation of even the worst of these in his unpleasant countenance.

'If you are interested in horses, perhaps you would like to see a trial?' he said.

The man's eyes sparkled.

'That would be a great honour,' he said. 'For what race is this trial?'

'The Stewards' Cup,' said Tony, to his trainer's amazement. 'I have two horses in the race; I am going to put them together with three or four others and let them come at racing pace for six furlongs. You will be able to see with your own eyes which horse is more likely to win.'

He saw suspicion dawn for an instant in those cunning eyes behind the thick lenses.

'That will be great fun,' said Mr. Guelder, and trotted amiably by the side of Tony's ambling hack.

They came at last to where half a dozen horses were walking in a circle, and Mr. Guelder stood aside and watched with eager interest the stripping of cloths and the final preparations. Two of the horses were led, and Tony very kindly told him their names, though there was no necessity in the case of one of them.

'That is Barley Tor, who I believe has been well backed for the race; the other is a very fast filly called Lydia Marton. She's a three-year-old. If you study racing, you probably know her history. She did not run till the spring of this year and she won a small race at Pontefract.'

'You wait for something now?' asked Mr. Guelder, deferentially.

'The jockeys. Here they are, I think.'

Tony looked down the road to where a cloud of dust followed on the trail of a powerful car, which pulled up near to where the horses were walking. Two slim, small figures got out; one wore gaiters and riding breeches, the other Jodhpurs, and Mr. Guelder recognized them both as two of the leading jockeys of the turf. One was a man of over thirty, dark, eagle-faced, sardonic of speech.

'I want you to ride Lydia Marton, Burnie,' said Tony Braid.

The second of the jockeys was already mounted on Barley Tor. They watched them canter down to the starting-post, and

Mr. Rex Guelder's brain was very busy. He knew Tony Braid, knew his reputation better. There was no love lost between Tony and Julian Reef, and his association with Julian was commonly known. It was extremely unlikely that Braid should be ignorant of the fact. Why, then, should he be inviting him to witness an important trial? That was not The Twister's way.

'You're in Reef's office, aren't you, Mr. Guelder?' said Tony, suddenly.

'Yes, that is my good fortune,' said Rex, wondering what was coming next.

'I suppose he's terribly upset by poor Lord Frensham's death?'

Guelder shook his head with an assumption of melancholy.

'Ah, the poor fellow! His groans and sighs are terrible to hear; and also there are other causes for suffering. My lord owed poor Julian very large and considerable sums. But that would not hurt his feelings – he has the good heart. It is the so sudden loss of his uncle. What tragedy! To Julian money is nothing. He is bright, he is clever, he has the considerable future.'

'I dare say,' said Tony, drily. 'Is business well with you, Mr. Guelder?'

Rex Guelder shrugged his broad shoulders.

'In the City it is always ups and always downs; but we are a fortunate house. We have great reserves, we have holdings and wonderful properties, and our futures are immense.'

Tony lit a cigarette with great care. He neither smiled nor expressed by gesture or so much as a movement of an eyelid, his profound scepticism in the solidity of Julian Reef's business.

'Now, of course,' said Guelder, warming at the opportunity for making a confidant of so powerful a man as Braid, 'we are all at sevens and sixes, because of Lulanga Oils – how they fall! Yesterday evening at seven shillings and sixpence. We hold many we purchase at two pounts.'

Tony smiled.

'I doubt it,' he said, and shook his head gently.

'Pardon me, at thirty shillings,' corrected Guelder.

Again that shaking head and sceptical smile.

'At a pount perhaps – I am not sure. And now the Chairman

of the Company is dead, and who knows what the future may be? I often think—'

'Watch the horses,' warned Tony.

The trial field had started. Six black specks bunched together in the distance. The trainer stood, his stop-watch gripped to the prismatic glasses at his eyes. Nearer and nearer they came; Mr. Guelder shook with excitement as he glared down the 'course'. He could pick them out now without the aid of glasses: the dark bay Barley Tor was leading, the chestnut Lydia Marton half a length behind. He saw the jockey on Barley Tor sitting quite still, and then, when they were still less than fifty yards from where the watchers stood, the chestnut Lydia Marton shot to the front and as they passed them there was daylight between her and the Stewards' Cup favourite.

Mr. Guelder drew a long breath; his eyes danced with excitement; for he had noticed that the jockey on Barley Tor had scarcely moved on his horse.

'Well?' said Tony's voice.

Guelder blinked up at him.

'Wonderful!'

'Have you any doubt as to which is the better horse?' asked Tony, controlling his smile.

The other shook his head vigorously.

'Obviously Lydia Marton! What a horse! What a fast flier! I can see now mit my own eyes – I thank you, Mr. Braid.'

'I shall run them both, of course,' said Tony, carelessly, 'and you will be able to tell your friends how foolish they are to make Barley Tor favourite when the filly is so much his superior.'

'Exactly. I have your permission?'

Guelder was bursting with laughter. This Twister!

An hour later he was on his way back to town in his sports car. He had intended remaining over the week-end, but now there was no time to be lost. On Tuesday the Stewards' Cup would be run and already there was a strong market.

He burst in upon Julian Reef; and that ruddy-faced man was in the act of totalling his commitments. Julian looked up and frowned.

'Hullo! I thought you were away for the week-end?' he said.

Guelder made no immediate reply; he walked to the door,

opened it and looked out. The clerks' room was unoccupied, the staff was at lunch. He came back to the desk and drew up a chair to face his confidant.

'Often you have told me that horse races are foolish.'

'And often you have told me things that proved it,' said Julian sourly. 'You cost me more money last Ascot than I earned in the week!'

Mr. Guelder's smile was bland and triumphant.

'Now I tell you something,' he said, and, lowering his voice, he spoke without pause for five minutes.

Julian listened absorbed. No scheme which would hurt his enemy could receive too close an examination. He knew as much about racing as the average man; he was too much of a gambler not to be fascinated by its possibilities, and he realized the importance of the news which the Dutchman had brought to him.

'He must have a pretty low view of your mentality to try a crude trick like that. What is the price of the horse?'

Guelder pulled a paper out of his pocket and ran his finger down a list.

'Seven to one – the favourite. Here, my good Julian, is money for nothing.'

'You're sure it was a trial?' asked Julian. 'It may have been no more than a good gallop.'

Mr. Guelder smiled even more broadly, dived down into his capacious trousers pocket and produced a very large watch.

'This I had in my pocket: at the moment the flat falls for the trainer, it falls also for me. I start it – click! And when they pass me, I stop it – click! One minute eleven seconds and two-fifths of a second. The so-clever Mr. Braid! He does not suspect that this poor fool of a Hollander has in his pocket as good a stop-watch as his! That is my system, my dear fellow – time well compiled, so many seconds for conditions of ground and atmosphere.'

Julian looked at him with a frown.

'System? I knew you were a mug about horses, but I didn't know you were such an outrageous jackass that you backed horses systematically. Do you make money?'

Mr. Guelder shrugged, waving his fat palm airily.

'Hundreds on a year – I bet very small, a little pound here

and a little pound there, but in the end I always succeed.'

He lied as glibly to Julian as he lied to himself. Rex Guelder's little system cost him the better part of four thousand pounds a year, but it was not expedient or safe to reveal this fact.

'Obviously The Twister was trying to fool you,' said Julian, thoughtfully.

He pulled the telephone towards him and gave a number, and after his conversation he called yet another firm of bookmakers . . .

He left his office that night with a light step. He and his confederate stood to win a little over £14,000. They stood to lose £2,500, which was not as pleasant a thought to Julian, who in these days was finding it rather difficult to raise sufficient money to pay his clerks' salaries, and was tortured day and night with the recollection that he had, in a moment of temporary insanity, given Frensham a receipt for the shares which might be unearthed at any moment by the man controlling his estate.

10

TONY BRAID had finished his breakfast and, with a long black cigarette holder between his teeth, was reading his correspondence. He was conscious that somebody had entered the room, but did not look up until he heard a laugh and his name spoken. He lifted his head with a jerk.

'Good lord! What on earth are you doing here?'

'I've driven up from Somerset,' said Ursula. 'I'm terribly bored, Tony. You see, my Somerset friends are relations of my father and they're rather inclined to feel that I should not read cheerful books 'or be amused. Poor dears! They are terribly mournful, but I think that's a normal condition with them.'

She looked very pretty and distressingly young. The usually pale face was tinted pink by her run through the morning air.

'Are you going back?'

She sighed and nodded.

'I'm afraid I must. I had to tell the most outrageous lie to get away at all. The butler is the only cheerful creature in the place, and he'll be doubly so if your tip wins!'

'There's no doubt about my tip winning,' smiled Anthony. And then, 'Have you had breakfast?'

She had taken coffee at Oxford, she said. He rang the bell and ordered her something more substantial.

'All the newspapers are filled with your Barley Tor. Why are you running two horses?' she asked.

'Because I'm a twister,' said Tony. 'And Mr. Rex Guelder would be very much disappointed if I didn't.'

She frowned at this.

'I hate that man. There's something horrible about him, Tony.'

'Do you know him?' he asked, remembering she had made a previous reference to the Dutchman.

'He came to the house once or twice, and I've never known so acute a discomfort of mind as I do in his presence. No, he was not offensive at all, he's most polite. He once kissed my hand, but that was only his Continental manner, and I didn't mind that at all. It's something about him that only a woman can understand, I suppose. You feel the rawness of his mind and it sort of grates on you. Julian says that he's very clever, in fact brilliant.'

'Have you heard from Julian?'

She shook her head.

'I don't think I'd like to hear from Julian,' she said quietly. 'We did not part on the best of terms. Perhaps I was wrong, Tony, but I told him that you and I had agreed not to inquire too deeply into my stock. Poor Father! Somebody told me that his precious Lulanga shares were selling at a ridiculous price – five shillings or something.'

Anthony corrected her.

'They're not selling, they're being offered at that price,' he said. 'I should be very much surprised if you could get any real money for them. And it's all the more amazing because the last reports I read were most favourable. Everybody in the City is in the dark about them; there's a rumour that the wells have run dry, but we've had no confirmation of this, and certainly, from the little I know about oil, I should imagine that we should have had very good warning of that disaster.'

'We?' she said in surprise. 'I didn't know that you also were concerned with that unfortunate stock.'

He nodded slowly.

'Yes – not on my own behalf. You seem to forget that I am the executor and trustee of your father's estate. He had, I believe, an enormous block of shares, and I shall be very much surprised if you haven't, too.'

There was a long silence.

'Can you understand it, Tony? The more I think about it, the more it puzzles me. Why should Father commit suicide when he had your offer of help?'

'I don't think he ever read my offer of help,' said Tony, looking past her. 'The envelope and the cheque were found torn up in the wastepaper basket. It is inexplicable – for the moment.'

He changed the subject abruptly, asked her what were her immediate plans. She had set out with the full intention of not returning to Wells, and then she had changed her mind and decided that she would go back and be recalled by telegram – if Tony would only play the part of a conspirator.

'I think I shall stay on at the Hampstead house,' she said. She looked at her watch. 'You're going to Goodwood, of course? I think I will wait until you've gone, and have a bath in your wonderful bathroom – you're an awful sybarite, aren't you? – and then wend my way back to romantic Somerset lanes and the terrible tedium of Aunt Polly.'

He thought, in spite of her surface gaiety, she looked rather a forlorn figure, standing under the portico of his house and waving him farewell as he drove away. He did not know the secret of the legacy, or how long it might be deferred, but he was quite sure that, save for her diminutive income from her northern estate, Ursula Frensham was ruined; and she would be very difficult to help, he decided, unless . . .

He sighed heavily. He was getting sentimental, he told himself, and he really was forty, with more than half his lifetime over, and she was nearly twenty years younger. On one point he was perfectly certain: he would never ask her to sacrifice her youth and become his wife. That would not be fair. His task was to secure his future, and put on a good face to hide the bitterness of watching a rival succeed where he had not dared . . .

Only that successful rival must not be Julian Reef.

Almost the first person he met when he climbed Singleton Hill and came to the beautiful course was Elk. He was standing near the paddock gates, the stub of a cigar in his mouth and a look of settled melancholy upon his unhappy face. He watched Tony get out of his car without making any signs of recognition, and Tony, believing that he did not wish to be spoken to, would have passed him.

'Hi, Mr. Braid! What's going to happen to me next week? I got fourteen pounds on your unbeatable certainty. You meant well by sending it, but if anybody can kill your horse dead, it's me. I never backed a winner in my life. The moment I put on money the horse turns round and goes the other way. I suppose he's heard about my bet.'

He jerked his head towards the paddock.

'Some friends of yours inside – sorrowing nephew and partner. I didn't see either of them crying, but I did read your famous letter in the Sporting Press.'

'Good lord!' said Tony, in surprise. 'Did they print it?'

He had forgotten all about the letter he had so carefully composed and despatched by special messenger to Fleet Street.

'Did they print it? They put it on the front page!'

Elk pulled a newspaper from his pocket, unfolded it, and pointed to a headed column:

'We have received the following from Mr. Anthony Braid, the owner of two of today's contestants in the Stewards' Cup. To the Editor of the *Sporting Times*:

DEAR SIR,—I note that the ring has made my horse Barley Tor favourite. I feel it is only right to the sporting public that they should know I intend running both horses on their merits, and that my filly, Lydia Marton is a little the better at the weights. I am not suggesting that either will win, or that Barley Tor may not do better on the racecourse than he does on his home gallop, but I feel it my duty to put the racing public in possession of the facts.'

There followed an editorial note!

'Mr. Anthony Braid is a very shrewd judge of racing, and his views, especially about his own horses, are to be respected. But, judging by past form, there can be little doubt that Barley Tor has the better credentials.'

'How will they bet?' asked Tony, as he handed the paper back.

Mr. Elk relit his cigar stump before he replied:

'Such is the confidence of the general public in you, Mr. Braid, that you no sooner started "knocking" Barley Tor than the ring made him a good favourite. He's at five to two.'

As Tony strolled across the paddock towards the weighing room, he heard a man say:

'That's him. The Twister!'

Many men would have been embarrassed. Tony was amused. He knew just who were the propagandists responsible for his evil reputation.

Not until he returned to the paddock did he see Julian, who greeted him with an affable smile, and came leisurely towards him. Julian was in his most amiable mood.

'I don't often come racing, Braid, but I thought I'd take a day off – I've backed your horse.'

'I'm delighted,' said Tony without enthusiasm. 'And which of my representatives has the honour of breaking his heart to win you a few pounds?'

Julian smiled cryptically. He felt at the moment he was entitled to amusement.

'You've backed your horse, of course – both of them?'

'One of them,' replied Tony, deliberately. 'I have a thousand pounds on Lydia Marton. Every penny of it will be put on at starting price and I think I shall go home from twelve to fourteen thousand pounds richer than when I came.'

Julian laughed. At that moment an acquaintance of both came up. He greeted Julian with a nod and devoted his attention to the owner of Barley Tor.

'I hear your horse was beaten in a trial – Barley Tor, I mean? They say Lydia Marton won it. Which do you fancy?'

'Lydia Marton,' said Tony, evading the questioner's eyes. He heard the inquirer grunt incredulously.

'He doesn't seem to believe you, Braid.'

Tony became aware that the man he disliked most of all people on earth was still with him.

'No. Queer, isn't it? It's a case of giving a dog a bad name and hanging yourself!'

Guelder was waiting at the paddock entrance a little impatiently for the return of his friend, and as they walked leisurely to the stand the Dutchman asked:

'What did he say?'

'The old tale,' said Julian. 'Really, that fellow is crude!'

Mr. Rex Guelder rubbed his fat cheek thoughtfully.

'Yet that is the kind of crudeness I had not noticed before in him, either by hearsay or acquaintanceship. With my own eyes I saw this trial,' he said, brightening, 'and do I not understand horses?'

They climbed on to the stand to see the field go down to the post, and Guelder pointed out the two horses, not to be mistaken one for the other. Lydia Marton carried the first colours which is usually the only indication an owner gives the public of his personal fancy.

'I will tell you how this race will be run,' said Mr. Guelder, confidently. 'First we shall see a pretence of the Lydia horse being in front. Then, like a flash, will come the Barley Tor, and that will be the end of the race!'

Julian was looking round disparagingly at the crowd which filled Tattersalls; and presently he saw Braid on the members' lawn.

'How the devil that fellow gets into a reserved enclosure at Goodwood beats me,' he said irritably. 'At any rate, when this race is over, his name will be mud with a very large section of the public. I've told everybody I know in the City to back Barley Tor.'

There was a roar from the crowd; glasses were turned down

the course . . . Before the inexperienced Julian Reef could pick out the colours, the horses were half-way home. Braid's two were racing side by side and they were clear of the field. And then he saw the chestnut draw ahead, seemingly without an effort. She was two lengths ahead of her stable companion when she passed the post.

11

GUELDER stared aghast.

'I saw it,' he said, thickly. 'Mit my own eyes. I saw it. My Gott! I am brainless! My frient' – he turned, but Julian was no longer at his side. He was pushing his way savagely through the crowd. On every hand he heard the inevitable comment.

'. . . Well, he told you this was the best horse . . . what more can you want . . .?'

By the ringside Tony received the congratulations – rueful, most of them – of his acquaintances.

'That was certainly a surprise, Braid.'

'It was a twist,' said Anthony calmly. 'I told the truth about the trial and about the relative merits of the horses – you had the truth; and the truth is a twist that very few people can understand!'

He saw Elk standing on the outskirts of the crowd, when it began to thin he approached the detective and in Mr. Elk's eye was a greater satisfaction than he ever remembered having seen.

'It was a bit of a temptation not to follow the money,' said Elk, 'but I didn't and now the money's following me. As a tipster you're in the first class, Mr. Braid, but I've just seen somebody who didn't have a good race. Mr. Reef looks as though a shaller depression was approachin' his shores – thunder and lightnin' expected shortly – and tornadoes. I'm going in to draw my money: they'll pay me because they know I'm at the Yard.'

'They'd pay you anyway, you old grouser,' smiled Tony. 'Why do you pretend everybody in the world is a crook?'

'They're not,' said Mr. Elk promptly. "*I'm* straight!'

Julian Reef had parked his car by the side of the road which leads down to Singleton. Here he waited for half an hour in a rage of impatience for the appearance of the Dutchman. Guelder came eventually, as cheerful as though he had never experienced the vicissitudes of fortune.

'Ach! That was bad!' he said, as he got into the car. 'Dat Twister! And mit my own eyes I saw the trial!'

'What is the matter with you is that you're too damned clever,' snarled Julian, as he jerked in his gear and sent the car rocking along the uneven surface of the road. 'I suppose you realize you've cost me more money than I can find on Monday?'

'Then, my frient, do not find it,' said Guelder unperturbed. 'Bookmakers are not settling day. Before you can be seriously inconvenienced there will be fortune enormous, incomparable.'

Julian glanced at his companion sideways and saw him lighting a long, thin and evil-smelling cigar.

'Is that going to be another of your winners?' he asked, sardonically. 'I've lived on promises and I've spent a fortune on your experiments, Guelder. I want a little back.'

'You shall have the lot,' smirked Guelder. 'Millions und millions! Soon I shall be able to say to you "Go to the market and take away money"!'

'Soon, soon!' said the other impatiently. 'When is soon?'

Guelder shrugged his broad shoulders.

'In a week, perhaps. My experiments are successful. Tonight or some other night I will make the final test, and then you shall come down and see for yourself.'

Julian said no word all the way back to town; he dropped Guelder at Victoria and went on to his own flat to spend an uneasy evening.

There was reason enough for his troubled mind. Frensham's papers had been impounded and in a few days they would be handed to Tony Braid for examination. That morning before he left he had received a notification from Frensham's lawyers, asking him to make an appointment with Tony to go into the affairs of Lulanga Oils. Frensham had controlled this company from his office in St. James's Street. He was, at the time of his death, the owner of nearly 200,000 shares, a fact which surprised Tony; but there was no mystery about this big holding. Julian Reef had once held a bigger block, but for reasons which had yet to be revealed he had off-loaded the bulk of the shares; and since the only genuine buyer in the market had been Frensham, with his blind faith in the future of the company, they had gravitated to his safe.

The value of the stock was indicated when the banks refused to accept even 200,000 as security against an overdraft. Their nominal price in the market had fallen to a few shillings, but there was no dealing. If Julian had attempted to sell the remaining 100,000 which he held, he would have found it impossible now that the only buyer of the stock had died.

Lulanga was a West African share. The oilfields had been discovered in Northern Angola and had been put on the market by men who had made a very great fortune from their flotation. Gradually the shares had sunk and sunk, until after Frensham's biggest purchase they had dropped from 38s. to something well under £1. This was the most puzzling. It puzzled the City, puzzled even the oil experts, in view of the very promising report by the engineer, a man respected in the City. There were cynical financiers who pointed out the peculiar fact that the report had not been published until a fortnight after the death of the engineer in question. He had been a cautious man and had never before been responsible for so optimistic a prophecy as was contained in his statement.

Julian put the matter out of his mind, as he did all uncomfortable thoughts; he set himself to compose a letter to Ursula Frensham that would, he hoped, do much to restore her confidence in him.

Half-way through the draft of the letter his fountain-pen ran dry, and he searched his drawer in vain for the ink. Then he remembered that Guelder would have some and he went into his office. The Dutchman had not closed down his roll-topped desk. Julian threw it up and searched the top of the desk, but there was no ink. He pulled out one drawer after another, and came to the bottom drawer . . .

Ursula Frensham's face stared up to him. It was a portrait he had seen a long time ago, but somebody had decorated it with a border of cupids and hearts. The draughtmanship was good. At first he thought that the border was printed and then he saw in the left-hand corner the initial of the artist.

Guelder! It was incredible. Was this a bad joke on the part of the Dutchman?

He lifted out the photograph and found another beneath it, undecorated except by what was obviously a poem, though as it was in Dutch, it was unintelligible.

Turning it over he found what was either a translation or a new flight of the Dutchman's fancy, in English!

> Beloved eyes that smile on me,
> Sweet lips that breathe of Araby . . .

He read it through, aghast. Guelder? It was incredible! And yet – he knew the man's reputation; had heard rumours of certain unsavoury happenings.

He shook with fury as he took out the contents of the drawer, forgetting for the moment the reason for the search. He tore the photographs to fragments and threw them into the wastepaper basket. He was outraged by the discovery. That this crude man should look upon Ursula in this way was revolting to him . . .

The next morning, when Guelder arrived, very bright and perky, with a smile and a wave of his fat hand for his chief, Julian stopped him.

'I went to your desk last night,' he said; 'I was looking for some ink—'

'It is on the shelf behind the desk—' began Guelder, but Julian stopped him.

'I am not concerned about that. I found some photographs in your drawer of Lady Ursula Frensham. Somebody had had the damned nerve to draw hearts and cupids around them!'

Rex Guelder's face went redder, his eyes seemed to sink to the back of his head.

'I was dat somebody,' he said harshly. 'Dat is my business what I haf in my desk!'

'Your business, eh? Well, I've made it mine,' said Reef,

brusquely. 'You'll be interested to know that I've torn them up and chucked them into the wastepaper basket.'

He watched the face of the Dutchman go from red to white; the man was blinking down at him, his thick lips twisted in a mirthless smile. He was fighting hard to control himself, and he succeeded.

'That was foolishness, my friend. They did no harm and they lightened my days. The young lady is very beautiful – I am a connoisseur. I suppose you would rather haf me sent them to Mynheer Braid?'

'I don't care a damn where they were sent,' said Julian. 'Braid is a gentleman, and you're a foul swine! I'm not picking my words with you, Guelder. I know your reputation, I know why you left Amsterdam in such a hurry and I've heard a few rumours about what happened in the Dutch East Indies. You're useful to me – at present an expensive luxury – but if you come into my business deals you do not come into my domestic affairs: you understand that?'

Guelder was breathing heavily; his face was tense, diabolical; it was now distorted with fury.

'So, so!' he said huskily. 'I am a schwine, yes? Good for your nasty businesses, but not for your lady friends to adore, eh? I make you millions and yet I am your servant – so!'

'You've made me very few millions up to now, Guelder. You've cost me a packet,' said Julian Reef.

The man interrupted him, leaning over the table and pointing his fat forefinger almost into his face.

'Ah! You say I must not think of Lady Ursula because I am too lowly, too – what is your word? – foul! Now shall I tell you somet'ing? That night Frensham shoot himself, eh? I haf plenty of time in town. I walk about admiring all der pretty girls. Then I see you and I am curious. I wonder where my frient the great Julian Reef shall be going. I follow you: you do not know. I watch you from eight o'clock till nine. You do not know that. I walk behind you, across the Bridge of Westminster. You lean over carelessly: somet'ing falls in der water. But somet'ing you drop does not fall in der water! One certain thing I find mit my own hands, resting on a leetle parapet!'

He held up his hand significantly, and Julian's face was as

white as death. He could only glare at the leering devil who was waggling his stubby fingers derisively.

'Those t'ings I haf in my leetle safe at Greenwich. I put them in my pocket, and when I come to my beautiful home I examine them and put them in my little safe. Some day,' – he wagged his finger so close to Julian's pallid face that he could feel the wind of it – 'some day this Julian may talk of Ursula Frensham; then I shall say "No, not for you, but for me, this beautiful piece of loveliness." You have destroyed my lovely pictures, but happily I have more in my home. If I had not, I should have said to you "Replace all you have destroyed, iconoclast"!'

He paused, out of breath, his face set in a malicious grin, but Julian said nothing. His face was a blank. Only in his glowing eyes did hatred show. There were questions he would have asked, but he dared not question this triumphant man – some acts would not endure the discovery of speech.

He did not expect that Rex Guelder would become suddenly conciliatory, and yet that was the Dutchman's immediate attitude.

'Do not let us discuss these unpleasant things; let us forget them. Just so that we understand each odder, dat is all dat is necessary. You need me, my frient – I need you. We are the ideal combination. With us is the future, the great fortune. All the night I have been planning for you and now my mind is organized – completely! You shall consolidate your respectful interests. There must be no breath of scandal. We must find money – I will find money – so that people shall not whisper into one another's ears, "This Reef is broken of cash"!'

Julian Reef licked his dry lips and steadied a voice that was inclined to be tremulous.

'Where is the money to come from?'

Guelder beamed at him.

'Who is this person who gives sixty-five or seventy-five thousand pounds to the bankrupt Lord Frensham? Who but the twisting Braid? He shall heap the war chest high! Little knowing that he is the enemy against whom we fight!'

Julian regarded the man with cold contempt.

'Do you imagine that Tony Braid will lend you or me large sums of money?'

The other nodded.

'Then you've got another guess coming, my friend. Braid would not raise the price of a rope to hang me.'

Guelder chuckled, and waggled his thick finger cunningly.

'Ah, I have every matter definitely arranged! It requires only that our friend should continue with his horse-racing and should not bodder with Lulanga Oils for another few weeks.'

The clerk came in at that moment with a telegram. It was addressed to Julian, and he opened it without any undue haste and glanced at its contents. Guelder saw his brows meet.

'That's coincidence,' said Julian Reef.

Guelder took the telegram from his hand and read:

I wish to go into the position of the Lulanga Oil Company tomorrow at ten at Frensham's office in St. James's Street.

It was signed *Anthony Braid*.

The two men looked at one another, and Guelder shook his head.

'Dat is very unfortunate,' he said. 'Extremely unfortunate!'

12

TONY was at the office in St. James's Street by nine o'clock the next morning. The staff of Lulanga Oils consisted of three girls, typists, and an old accountant who had been associated with Frensham in one capacity or another half his lifetime.

'I have put all the documents concerning the company on your desk, Mr. Braid,' he said. 'I am afraid you will find we have had a rather haphazard method of conducting our business. The share transfer books, however, have been kept in good order: I myself have seen to that.'

Tony had not been engaged for very long in examining the correspondence of Lulanga Oils before he realized that 'haphazard' was rather a flattering term to apply to Lord Frensham's method of doing business. He found unopened letters (one of which contained a cheque for hundreds of pounds) and scores of letters which had called for immediate attention, but which – according to the accountant, who was also book-keeper – had never been attended to.

'His lordship disliked dealing with anything unpleasant,' said Main, the old clerk, 'and since the shares have been dropping he has hardly done more than glance at any of the correspondence I have placed before him.'

Tony nodded; he had had acquaintance with that peculiar mentality.

'Didn't Mr. Reef do some work at this office?' he demanded.

Main hesitated.

'No; his lordship was rather impatient of interference, and although I think Mr. Julian was very willing to help, his lordship gave him no encouragement. What often happened was that if anything serious came to hand, and I could not secure Lord Frensham's attention I would take the matter into the City to Mr. Julian. And he *did* attend to most of the correspondence between the South African office and ourselves.'

Tony made no comment: the more he saw of the muddled state of Frensham's affairs, the more readily he could believe the story that the clerk told him.

He had not got a sixth of the way down the pile of correspondence when Julian arrived, in his most cheerful and most amiable mood.

'I'm terribly sorry if I'm late,' he said.

He had under his arm a big portfolio which contained documents relating to the company.

'Nothing of any great importance,' he said, and glanced at the pile at Tony's left elbow. 'Have you finished with the accumulation?'

'Not yet,' said the other. 'What are those?'

Julian flourished a handful of papers.

'Just a few letters. Really they relate to affairs which I have settled on Frensham's behalf.' He put them on the table by the side of the other papers. 'He used to keep quite a lot of papers relating to the company in a black japanned box in the inner office.'

'I've opened all the boxes,' said Tony.

'But not the Lulanga box, surely?'

Anthony went into the inner office and examined the deed boxes which had been unlocked. With one exception, they were empty, and even the exception contained nothing that related in the slightest degree to Lulanga Oils. He came back to find Julian looking out of the window.

'Good Lord, this would be an easy place to burgle,' he said. 'Look at that fire-escape right under the window!'

'Your views are shared by a very eminent member of the Metropolitan police force,' said Tony drily. 'Mr. Elk — I think you have heard of him?'

'Yes, I know him. I can't say that I am particularly friendly with him. The fact is, I had a slight fracas — a wordy one, it is true, but none the less upsetting.'

He did not particularize the cause of the quarrel he had had with Elk, and which Tony was now hearing about for the first time.

Julian turned from the window and sat down opposite this hateful man.

'What are you going to do? I think the best thing is to burn them,' he said.

'A very simple solution,' replied Tony quietly. 'I prefer, however, to go through them one by one. There are sure to be many of them here on which you can enlighten me.'

Julian Reef nodded, took a gold case from his pocket and lighted a cigarette, watching curiously and with every evidence of unfriendliness the monotonous business of checking up the letters and documents one by one. Out of the corner of his eye he saw Tony Braid take up two closely typewritten sheets of foolscap which were fastened together by a metal stamp.

'Hullo! What's this?' said Tony wonderingly, as he read the first words.

Half-way down the page he turned to the bottom of the next to make sure if he knew the writer.

'This is from the resident engineer in charge of the working end of the Lulanga fields,' he said slowly. 'Are you a director of Lulangas?'

Julian shook his head.

'No, I resigned my directorship a few days before Frensham's death,' he said glibly.

Tony's disbelieving eyes were fixed upon the face of the man.

'Frensham did not tell me this,' he said.

'I doubt if anybody else in the company knows it. You'll probably find my letters among the correspondence. The fact is, Braid,' he went on in an outburst of frankness, 'I got rather tired of my uncle's folly. I've been advising him to sell these shares for months. But, of course, if I kept my own off the market—'

'You had a very simple method of keeping your own off the market,' said Tony. 'You seem to have passed them on to Frensham – it was he who was your private baby holder, I presume? I've already seen a transfer of a very large block of shares from your books to his.'

Julian lifted his shoulders with a deprecating glance.

'What am I to do? I can't take risks – not the kind of risk he wanted me to take, at any rate. What is that?' he asked, with well-simulated curiosity.

Tony had read the preamble and now was engrossed in the document. It began:

A report on Shafts 15, 16 and 18, Lulanga Oil Wells, Majasaka, West Africa.

MY LORD, Owing to the loss of mail bags addressed to this part of the world, I have missed two weekly issues of my report to your Lordship concerning the above wells. I imagined that the Company would lose no time in publishing this rather disquieting news, but the latest journals to hand contain the information that Lulanga Oils are maintaining their price. As I wrote previously, these three wells showed signs of drying up, and the first and second of these are now out of use. Borings have been conducted at 85, 97 and 132 on T plan, but so far without satisfactory results. I should not be doing my duty if I failed to inform the Board that in my judgement

Lulanga Oils are no longer a marketable proposition. The
Board will remember that since I have taken over my duties
from Mr. Colburn I have taken nothing but a pessimistic
view of the Company's prospects, and these, I regret to say,
have been fully justified by the latest developments . . .

'Colburn?' The name seemed familiar. And then, in a flash,
Tony remembered Elk's erratic fellow-boarder. 'Who was
Colburn?' he asked.

'Oh, he was a fellow we dismissed for drunkenness and
general incompetence. He got a job somewhere else on the
coast. I don't know what became of him.'

Tony handed the report to the younger man and Mr. Reef
read, his eyes opening wider and wider, his eyebrows rising,
so that any stranger who had no knowledge of the circumstances might well have thought that he was receiving the
surprise of his life.

'This is the most amazing thing I have ever read,' he began.

'Never seen it before?'

The question came like the crack of a whip.

'Why should I have seen it before? Obviously it was
addressed to Frensham. That was one of the fool things he
would do. He hated trouble of any kind . . . this is most
serious . . .'

'You've never seen it before?' asked Tony again, and a
deeper red came into Julian's face.

'What the hell do you mean?' he asked. 'I've told you I've
never seen it before in my life. Do you imagine that I would
allow a thing like this to be suppressed?'

Tony pursed his lips thoughtfully, his eyes never leaving the
other's face.

'A few months ago, after the death of the engineer, a statement was issued by the company purporting to be signed by
this man. Who issued it?'

Julian thought quickly. Here at least he could not lie! The
facts were too easy to prove.

'I issued it,' he said boldly.

'Had you seen the document in question?'

Again Reef considered.

'Yes,' he said.

'Have you the original report of the engineer saying that the prospects in the field were never better – that which you published?'

Julian drew a long breath; his eyes did not waver.

'No, I haven't the original. It was sent to me to copy. I believe I sent my typewritten copy to the printer. Obviously, Frensham—'

'Do you suggest that Frensham would send out a forged report and suppress the truth about this mine?' And when he did not answer, Tony went on relentlessly: 'You know Frensham much better than I. Did he ever do a dirty trick in his life, or a crooked thing? Was he capable of swindling the public deliberately and feloniously?'

Julian shrugged his shoulders.

'How do I know?' he asked. 'Of course, he was a very sound fellow and all that sort of thing, but who knows another man's secret heart? The only thing I am certain about is that I have never seen this report before, but I did see the report which was signed by the engineer saying that the prospects were good – probably he had reasons—'

Tony silenced him with a gesture.

'I'll tell you something, Reef.'

He was standing up now, leaning over the table, his knuckles on the blotting-pad. 'This report you just read was not amongst Frensham's documents till you came.'

'What do you mean?' demanded Julian, breathing heavily.

'I mean that I went through the whole pile of correspondence, and if I've no memory for some things, I've an excellent memory for others; and one of those is colour. There was no document typed on light blue paper, as this is.'

A dead silence followed.

'What are you suggesting?' Julian found his voice at last.

'I am suggesting that when I went into the other room, at your suggestion, in search of purely mythical documents, you slipped that report amongst the papers. I'm not only suggesting it, I'm stating it.'

Julian Reef looked his panic fear, he did not speak. His nerves were already shaken when he had come. The tremendous and unspoken accusation of Guelder had left him a moral wreck.

'Not only did you put that report amongst the papers, but it was you who forged the engineer's report that sent up Lulanga Oils to 17s. I've not discovered much in this office, but one thing I have learned – all the correspondence from Africa you dealt with. It is a very simple matter, Reef, to discover how many shares you sold on the top of that forged report of the company's prosperity, and a simple matter to put you where you belong. Do I make myself clear?'

Julian did not reply.

'I could call in a detective and charge you right away. I have sufficient evidence to send you to prison for seven years. But I'm not going to do it. Do you know why? I want to keep Frensham's name clean. I don't want your dirty accusation that he was responsible for this trickery to be thrashed out in open court. That is just what saves you.'

Julian forced a smile.

'And Ursula, one supposes . . . What nonsense you're talking, Braid! You couldn't possibly charge me. There isn't a single act of mine provable. And for a good reason,' he went on quickly, 'because I'm perfectly innocent. I don't know whether Frensham was a crook or whether he was straight – that is not my business. All I know is that he authorized the issue of the report, and that I've never seen this engineer's letter before.'

'In other words, that he deliberately suppressed it?'

Julian Reef saw the danger, and literally backed out.

'I'm not saying that; I am merely anticipating what the world would say, what the average man in the street would say.'

Tony pointed to the door.

'Be a man in the street yourself, will you – and damned quick!'

Julian did not think it was a moment to argue. He left – a man so enraged, so mortified that he was near to tears when he came out into the blinding sunlight of St. James's Street.

13

THE neat messenger at Scotland Yard came back to Tony with the information that Mr. Elk would see him. Tony followed the official up many flights of stairs and along interminable corridors and came at last to a very tiny room and to a sprawling Elk.

'Come in, Mr. Braid. Shut the door, messenger, will you? Do you mind coming farther into the room so that he can shut the door? It's the smallest room in Scotland Yard. I'm nobody. The Chief Commissioner will be making a cage and hanging it out of the window for me one of these days.'

He rose and offered Tony the one chair the office boasted.

'It's all right. I always sit on the table; it's more dignified,' said Elk. 'I suppose you haven't got a cigar with you . . .? Thanks, I left my case at home – some other fellow's home. They were his cigars. When that messenger came and said there was a gentleman to see me, I thought it was a burglar friend of mine with a squeak. But you'll do. What do you want, Mr. Braid? Have you been swindled by your bookmaker? The worst of these credit accounts is you never know whether you're up or down till Saturday. Now I got mine in ready cash —'

'What has happened to Mr. Colburn?' asked Tony.

Elk stared at him.

'My brother lodger – don't tell me he's got into trouble.'

'Is he still staying in your house?'

Elk nodded.

'Sure! When he's asleep. That's the only time he ever stays anywhere!'

'Do you think I could see him? You remember I asked you to bring him to Ascot.'

Elk scratched his chin and glanced at the clock.

'Ascot's a pretty long way,' he said.

'I don't want him at Ascot really; I can see him in London. Could you bring him after dinner?'

Elk nodded, but the visitor could see he was a little doubtful.

'Oh yes, if I can find him,' he said, in answer to Tony's

question. 'But he's what I might call a gregarious man, and once he gets into sociable company . . . well . . . I mean he can't carry good liquor. What wouldn't do more than raise my drooping courage, if you'll forgive the poetical expression, makes *him* talk about being the rightful heir of the duke.'

'In other words, he may be a little drunk. I don't mind that. Bring him along.'

Elk nodded again; but he was doubtful.

'He shall come if I have to bring him in an ambulance,' he said. And then, looking out of the window and apparently indulging in a chance thought, 'You've been casting up accounts this morning, they tell me?'

'Who on earth told you that?'

'A little bird,' he said. 'It's a pity about poor young Reef. He was quite upset, wasn't he? I saw him on St. James's Street with tears running down his face. Poor feller! It must be awful to lose an uncle. I had one, but I could never lose him. That man could find his way home in a fog even if the roads were up.'

Tony was on the point of departure, but now he came back.

'Were you watching the office?' he asked.

The detective's face was a study in hurt innocence.

'I never watch anything,' he said. 'Not for long. It makes me dizzy. What I like to study is life, passing hither and thither, as it were.'

'But who told you that I was going over Frensham's documents?'

Mr. Elk raised his eyes to the ceiling and seemed to be thinking hard.

'I forget now. I've got an idea it was that antique clerk of Frensham's. What's his name again – Main. I was having a cup of tea in a respectable teashop when he came and sat down at the same table.'

'Or you came and sat down at his table?' suggested Tony.

'It may be,' agreed the other. 'A very nice fellow – he keeps chickens. I know another fellow who used to keep chickens – I went to his execution. Mr. Braid, have you got anything running at Brighton next week? I like racing! It gives you a day in the air.'

Tony left Scotland Yard more than a little puzzled. He

would have been more puzzled if he had heard the instructions that Inspector Elk was giving to the subordinate whom he had summoned to his tiny room.

'Watch Mr. Braid; don't let him out of your sight. I'll arrange to relieve you at eight o'clock tonight.'

14

AFTER all, Ursula had come back to London on her own initiative and without the subterfuge of telegrams or excuses, except that she had not told her mildly indignant relatives that she was utterly bored. They had already decided she was more than a little heartless, possibly eccentric, very likely fast. They raised their eyebrows after she had gone, and looked at one another meaningly, but nobody knew what the other meant, which is quite understandable, since they did not know themselves.

It required some courage to take in hand the rearrangements of the house, to move familiar objects so closely associated with her dead father. She had his own two rooms closed and dismantled. Perhaps there would come a time when she could use them, but for the moment they stood for tragedy and heartache.

Only one happy person had she left at Wells; the saintly-looking butler carried her bag to the car and in an agitated undertone expressed his gratitude for her help and advice.

'I've got a hundred to six to nine pounds, miss, and I'd take it very kindly if you would thank Mr. Braid, and if you would be good enough, miss, to ask him if his two-year-old has any chance at Lewes . . . Not that I want to trouble you, miss.'

'I'll be sure to ask him,' she assured the anxious man, and left him bowing – a portly churchwarden of a man, who ran two s.p. accounts in London and a ready-money arrangement with a bookmaker in Glasgow.

Racing was beginning to interest her in a faint way. She was surprised how far extended was the interest of the sport; she discovered that she had acquired a new importance, not only in the eyes of the servants, but with the tradesmen of Wells since Lydia Marton had won the Stewards' Cup – for the butler had not been at all reticent after he had taken his own bet.

Happily, when she returned home, there were no servants to be dismissed. Lord Frensham's household was a tiny one; he had never employed a valet – he said they fussed him. The domestic rearrangements were made with little or no trouble.

'I shall just keep the maid for as long as I can afford it,' she told Tony over the 'phone.

He wasn't so happy.

'I'm rather uneasy about you living in that house alone, with only a maid. You had better send your jewels to the bank.'

She scoffed at his solicitude, but in the end compromised by agreeing to do so.

There were other and more serious factors to be considered, so serious that all others hung upon them. She had taken stock of her own fortune and found it a meagre one. Her trip to Wells had also cleared up the mystery of the great legacy which would one day be hers. A cold-blooded clerk in holy orders, her second cousin, explained to her in great detail – for he had a passion for the law – that the legacy was rather a nebulous thing, since before it came to her three lives must pass, two of which were singularly young and healthy. She hadn't really considered this question of her future, being comforted by a dim knowledge that somewhere hovering in the misty background were enormous estates which would one day, in some manner painless to anybody else, be hers for the signing of a paper.

Tony came up to tea on the day she arrived, and she explained the exact position.

'And really I don't want these unfortunate second cousins twice removed to be completely removed from this world, Tony. I think we can wipe out that enormous legacy, and concentrate our hearts and minds upon getting me a job of work. I have taken lessons in shorthand and typing – that was

Father's idea – and I think I would make a most admirable secretary to some prosperous financier.'

'That isn't me,' said Tony promptly. 'I'll tell you one thing you have got,' he went on grimly. 'For some reason which I can't understand, Frensham transferred the whole of his Lulanga shares in your name. They were transferred on the day of his death.'

She frowned at this.

'Are they worth anything?' she asked.

'I should think they're worth absolutely nothing.' He hesitated. 'That is a brutal thing to say, but from what I gathered this morning, and from documents I have seen, I'm afraid they are everything except a liability. Thank heaven they are not that!'

She did not know how shares could be a liability, and he explained the mystery of called and uncalled capital.

'What did Julian say about them?' she asked suddenly.

He faced her squarely.

'It doesn't really matter what Julian said, Ursula. I don't want you to see Julian again, or to write to him.'

She looked at him for a long time without speaking, and then slowly inclined her head.

'Very well, Tony; I won't even ask you why – and that's the greatest compliment that I can pay to you. It isn't going to be very hard to drop Julian!'

There was a long pause, and the silence was a little painful to one of the two.

'What were you going to say, Tony?' she said, in a low voice; and then unaccountably dropped her eyes.

'I have quite a lot to say.' His voice was very steady. 'I wonder if you realize how terribly difficult it is for me to say nothing.'

He heard the half sigh; there and then he might have taken her into his arms and told her the one thing she guessed, the one thing indeed she knew, that he loved her. And yet it would not have been like him if he had, she told herself after he had gone. He would be afraid of himself, afraid of the reproach that he had caught her in an unguarded moment, when the reaction to her father's death had left her susceptible to attack.

Tony did not dine at home; he arrived at his house at a quarter past eight, prepared to wait until Elk and his erratic friend arrived. There had been no telephone message from the detective, which was encouraging. Yet it was not till some time after nine that Elk pushed before him into Tony's study the mysterious Mr. Colburn.

He was a very fat man, pink-faced, slightly bald, with blue staring eyes, and he sported a wispy ginger beard. He was rather noisy; but apparently this was a normal condition. His attitude was one of great frankness. He greeted Tony as a brother.

'Heard about you, Mr. Braid. Elk's friends are my friends! Excuse me tonight, but I've been having a friendly argument with an old Borstalian – a man of genius, without faith in life or hope of heaven!'

He chuckled at this and slapped his knee with a resounding thwack. Elk looked apologetic. His own attitude bespoke his sense of responsibility. For no particular reason, unless it was that he recognized the acoustic limitations of the room, Mr. Colburn dropped his voice.

'I'm sailing for the coast next week, Mr. Braid, and I meant to look you up, even if my dear old friend the copper hadn't brought me along. I might tell you I came to this country with twelve hundred pounds; and I'd have been twelve hundred minus by now if it hadn't been for the kindly fate which led me to his hospitable roof.'

His diction was stilted, and a trifle flamboyant. It was obvious that Mr. Elk admired this peculiar variety of eloquence.

'He was telling me you're interested in Lulangas.'

Tony nodded.

'I am – and curiously enough I discovered today that you were once the engineer of the company.'

'Assistant engineer and manager,' corrected the other. 'I'm not going to bluff you, Mr. Braid: I haven't the qualifications for a pukka engineer. I'm one of those superior mechanics, and not so darned superior! Self-educated, self-made and self-satisfied!'

This was evidently his stock joke. Elk began to smile mechanically before he had finished his sentence. Then he became sober again.

'No, I'm going back to Lulangas, but before I pop off I want to make a trade with anybody holding a block of shares – a block big enough to be worth while.'

'What kind of trade?' asked Tony, interested.

Colburn looked at him with a speculative eye.

'I don't know whether it's fair or not fair, but I want twenty thousand shares – for nothing! I know they're at junk prices on the market, and with a bit of luck I can get twenty thousand for a thousand pounds, but I'm not spending a thousand pounds.'

'And what does the giver of the twenty thousand receive in exchange?' asked Tony.

The man smiled expansively, almost pityingly, Tony thought.

'Oil,' he said, with a fine gesture. 'Thousands and maybe millions of tons of it!'

'From Well 16 and Well 18?' asked Tony, and Colburn laughed scornfully.

'They weren't wells, they were pinpricks into seepage! They've been boring since, they tell me. That consumptive engineer they took on after me's a clever fellow, but he works on textbooks – dead is he? . . . God rest him! He was a good fellow, but had no initiative. Such people often die. I wouldn't be talking to you, mister, but old Elk's strong for you. He says they call you The Twister —'

'No, I didn't,' said Elk loudly.

'What's the good of lying?' demanded the other, with a sad shake of his head.

'I said common people called him The Twister —'

'I'm a common man, but I know a straight 'un when I see him. Drunk or sober, nobody can twist me. All my cards are on the table to you, Mr. Lace —'

'Braid,' said Tony, gently.

Colburn was amused at his error.

'They kicked me off that property because I was slightly oiled, to use a local term. I went on a jag that lasted three weeks. A friend of mine on a German boat took me down to Mossamedes – anyway, you're not interested in my troubles –

but I know those Lulanga fields better than you know Regent Street. I know the ridge that runs across it. They call it the Pogolaki Mountain. Mountain! It's a dust heap! Give me a gang of a thousand men and I'd shovel it away in a year and leave a hole in the ground! All the borings are west of Pogolaki. I'm putting my cards on the table,' he said again. 'I'm trusting to you as a gentleman. The oil's on the east of Pogolaki. They won't even bore because it's sand, and there's no sign of shale, but I know more about oil than the average sardine. And you don't always find shale – nor surface shale – or you don't find it showing near the surface. Got a pencil and paper?'

Tony found them and the man made a very rapid and, as Tony guessed, an accurate sketch of the oilfield.

'The concession goes west and east of there, the M'ninga River – it's not a river, it's a puddle . . . there's no oil there. But come nearer to the ridge and you couldn't bore without striking a gusher. What's more, Mr. Braid, the company have got the equipment for boring and for dealing with any hell's amount of oil. They can siphon it over the ridge; the ground is covered with useless machines and ground tanks that could be utilized – the only thing is they haven't got the equipment to carry it away. The moment you started boring, you'd have to charter tankers – lot's of 'em!'

Was he speaking the truth? At any rate he believed it was the truth, Tony was convinced.

'How can you prove this?' he asked. 'If you can bring me proof that will satisfy me, I'll give you not twenty but thirty thousand shares.'

Mr. Colburn smiled.

'The only proof of oil is oil,' he said tersely. 'If you had proof, Lulangas wouldn't be selling at twopence ha'penny. I haven't asked you for money, have I? I haven't asked you even for a job – though you'll have to make me engineer and manager. I wouldn't even ask a salary for that. I'd stand pat on my twenty thousand or thirty thousand, and take my small commission. And I don't want money to pay my fare out, either, but I do want authority to work that field, and I haven't got it. Look at this!' He took out a handful of paper money and planked it on the table. 'There's eight hundred pounds cash there. I'm asking for nothing more than the privilege of making you a millionaire.'

'That seems fair,' murmured Elk.

The man had something yet to disclose, and presently it came out.

'You want proof? Well, you'll get it in a day or two! I'll tell you the truth, Mr. . . . Braid. I've been doing a bit of private boring on the edge of that property – me and a tough son of a gun who used to prospect with me, and two natives have been hand-boring for three months. I ought to be out there watching points, but I've hung on here, trying to get in big on the market. I went to see that fellow Reef the other day, but he was away somewhere, racing. He's got a lot of shares. Lord Frensham had a lot of shares – the chap who shot himself.'

'I have Lord Frensham's shares,' said Tony. 'When do you expect the proof?'

'Almost any day now. We've only got a primitive drill and that takes time. And naturally I'm getting no cables through, because they could only pass through the telegraph office on the Lulanga property.'

'In other words,' smiled Tony, 'you're doing a little bit of oil poaching?'

The man shook his head.

'Wrong – I've got a licence for all I've done – if you search the books of the company you'll find it – now is it a bet about my thirty thousand shares?'

'I'll sleep on it,' said Tony.

He walked to the door, saw the man into a taxi, and then took Elk aside.

'Impress upon your friend that the fewer people who know about this dream of his – supposing it is nothing else – the better.'

'If I'd had five thousand pounds —' began Elk.

'You haven't,' said Tony, 'but if I can buy you a few shares, and there's the faintest hope of their rising, I'll make you enough money to buy Scotland Yard.'

15

WHEN, two days later, a clerk came into Julian's office and announced that Mr. Braid wished to see him, Julian felt the inclination to say that he was not in.

'All right,' he said, and braced himself for what he believed would be a very unpleasant interview.

Tony, as usual, was immaculate. He took off his gloves and placed them in the interior of his hat before he sat down.

'How many Lulanga shares have you got?' he asked.

Julian drew a deep breath.

'Is this another inquisition? I thought I made it clear to you —'

'You made nothing clear to me about your own shares.'

'I've got a hundred thousand – or, to be exact, a hundred and ten thousand. Why? Have you discovered a new report?' he sneered. 'One that says the shares are going sky-high?'

'I've not discovered a new report' – Tony was choosing his words with the greatest care – 'nor have I invented one. But I think that there might be oil on the property yet. In which case the shares will be worth five times what they are today. If there is that possibility, I should like to have a controlling interest. I have two hundred thousand of Lord Frensham's – or rather, of Lady Ursula Frensham's. The share capital is six hundred thousand, and if I am going to make a profit, it is necessary that I should have that control.'

A light dawned on Julian. Not for nothing was this man called The Twister.

'I see,' he said. 'Your idea is to make a market, off-load your holding and get out at a profit, eh? That's what you call high finance, isn't it?'

'Of high finance I know nothing,' said Tony. 'Of low finance I have seen a little too much in the last two or three days. The question is, whether you're prepared to sell such Lulangas as you hold personally.'

Julian was not only prepared to sell, but was most anxious to rid himself of the incubus, and if Braid was sincere and really did wish to buy for hard cash, the money would be most acceptable. Money was needed very badly, for his new scheme was approaching its birth.

'At present the shares are well below their market value —' he began.

'I may publish the engineer's report tomorrow,' interrupted Tony; 'and then perhaps you will have a more definite view as to their market value.'

Julian Reef flushed angrily.

'That is to say, you're going to destroy whatever value the shares have. What is the idea, Braid?'

Tony shook his head.

'I'm not prepared to discuss my private plans. The point is, at what price are you prepared to sell?'

Julian thought quickly; he knew, to his sorrow, that it was practically impossible to dispose of Lulangas in the open market. He had offered his block only the day before for a sum equivalent to a few pence per share. He named a price, and saw Tony smile.

'Well, they're worth it,' he insisted; 'but if they're Ursula's shares —'

'I didn't say they were Ursula's shares, I said they were Lady Ursula Frensham's shares,' said Tony steadily. 'I could rather wish that you would not call her by her Christian name.'

For a second Julian showed his teeth.

'You're getting a little proprietorial, aren't you? However, I don't want to quarrel with you. You have your own ideas about Lulanga Oils, and possibly they are right. I have always had faith in the property, but you're dabbling in a strange field, Braid. I understood you were a diamond man? Oil fields are tricky things. I will sell you my block at six shillings, which is the price at which they were dealt in last.'

He never dreamt for one moment that the other would agree to a valuation which, in view of all he knew, was exorbitant.

'That's a stiff figure to pay for bone-dry wells,' said Tony, 'but I'll take them. Fix the transfer and I'll give you a cheque.'

Julian was staggered, and then the humour of the situation struck him and he laughed.

'You're a bold gambler,' he said good-humouredly, but he woke no smiling response in Anthony Braid.

It took exactly ten minutes to transfer all the Lulanga Oils he possessed to the other, and he had a very particular sense of satisfaction as he folded Tony's cheque and put it in his pocket.

'You know what you're buying, of course. You've seen the report, and this may interest you.'

From his desk he selected a cablegram and passed it across to his visitor.

'A month ago I sent an independent engineer out to report on the wells,' he said, 'and here it is.'

Tony read:

Output negligible. Most of the wells are dry. Those that are not are producing diminished quantities. Small boring under licence from this company going on east of ridge, in my opinion with very little hope of success.

'Thank you,' said Tony, as he handed back the telegram. He walked to the door and paused.

'If any of your friends have large holdings in this stock I shall be glad to take them off their hands,' he said.

'Why not try the Stock Exchange?' retorted Julian. 'It is one of those unimportant institutions about which you may not have heard? I've no doubt that if you want to add to your interesting collection, there are quite a number of shareholders who will oblige you.'

When Mr. Guelder came a little later he found his partner in a very amiable mood, and learned the reason. Guelder scratched his nose and was by no means elated.

'Hump!' he said. 'Dat Twister!'

He read the cablegram, which he had not previously seen.

'"Under licence": what is dat? Who bores on the other side of the ridge?'

Julian explained that the company were always prepared to give licences to prospectors who wished to test any other part of the property in the recognized oil area.

'There's nothing to it, anyway – they undertake to give us seventy-five per cent of their output and we market the oil. Frensham gave the licence some time ago to that fellow

Colburn, the man who used to be engineer on the property and was fired for being a soak.'

'Colburn?' The other looked up sharply. 'He came to the office three weeks ago, when you were away in Cornwall – a very noisy fellow.'

'I don't even know him,' replied Julian carelessly.

'He is in London, my frient. Has that no significance for you?'

'Even his being in London won't put oil into Lulanga,' chuckled Julian.

A quarter of an hour before lunch, Guelder came in from the clerk's office, a tape in his hand, closed the door behind him, and moving slowly to where Julian was sitting, laid the strip of paper before him.

'What is that?' said Reef, looking up.

'You shall read,' said the other.

Reef pulled the paper towards him, read and frowned.

'Lulanga Oils 17/9, 18/6, 18/9, 20/3.'

He stared incredulously. 'That crazy fool is buying!'

Guelder shook his head.

'There are several ways of being crazy,' he said, 'but this man could not go mad to his own hurt. He is a gambler, yes, but he does not gamble in the dark. Why not buy, my good Julian? If it is goot for him, is it not goot for you?'

'You may know a hell of a lot about science, but you have no knowledge of the market,' said Julian, angrily. 'Can't you see, you fool, they will be down to cat's meat prices before the house closes?'

His prophecy was not justified. The last quotation for the Lulanga Oils was 27s. 'There's a twist in it somewhere,' said Julian and he was almost right.

In the early morning, when he turned the pages of his newspaper in bed, he saw a headed paragraph:

SENSATION OF THE OILFIELDS
Dramatic rise of Lulangas. Worthless shares now valued at £2

Yesterday morning, people who held Lulanga oil shares bewailed their fate. This morning those who parted with their shares at low prices must be tearing their hair. Mr. Anthony Braid, whose activities have hitherto been confined to diamond propositions, was the chief buyer of Lulanga Oils. We understand that he took a block of over 100,000 from a well-known City man yesterday morning at 6s. By the end of the day he was considerably over £100,000 in pocket! Interviewed at his house last night, Mr. Braid said there was nothing remarkable about the rise. Independent prospectors boring on the edge of the property had tapped the true field. The results were amazing, the possibilities beyond computation. Mr. Colburn, the new engineer, was leaving on Saturday for the property, in response to a telegram from his foreman, who had been engaged in experimental boring...

Julian threw the paper on to the floor, his face livid with fury. Tony Braid had told him there was oil, had told him the shares were worth five times the price at which he had sold. That was the twist – the truth!

16

URSULA FRENSHAM sat like one in a dream. Her fortune was, then, a reality! She looked at Tony's letter again:

... If you will be advised by me, you will not sell a share. If Colburn's friends are right, they will be worth an enormous sum; if they are mistaken, it would be wrong to 'unload'. The only person who can be hurt if the story of the new gushers is unfounded is me, for I have been the chief and, I think, the only buyer. I got into the market and cleared off all that floated before some of my friends in the City were awake.

There were others who did not exercise the patience which Tony advised. A certain detective inspector of Scotland Yard, who had purchased a thousand, rang up his mentor three times in one morning, and finished up by coming in on Tony when he was eating his frugal lunch.

'It's the first time I've bought stocks and shares,' he said plaintively, 'and it's worrying me to death, Mr. Braid. Every time I look at the newspaper I get a feeling that I'm ruined. I'm beginning to understand why stockbrokers are not respectable. If anything will drive a man to crime, it's the market!'

Tony offered to take the shares from the hands of his friend at the current price. Mr. Elk was undecided.

'They might go up after that,' he said, 'and that'd make me so bitter I wouldn't be responsible for my actions. I'm getting into a fast City set, Mr. Braid. That's what stocks and shares lead you to. I got a whisper from a fellow yesterday – a high-up fellow, too – if I wanted to make money I must "bear" diamonds.'

Tony looked at him in amazement.

'Are you serious?'

'Fact,' nodded Elk; 'a big man.'

He mentioned the name. Tony recognized it as one of the few firms in the City that were friendly to Julian Reef.

'According to this man, diamond shares are going to tumble down. All you have to do is to sell a few you haven't got, and when the time comes to deliver 'em, pretend to buy the stock at a lower price. They've bought and never sold, but you get the difference. It's the most attractive form of larceny I know.'

Here was food for thought, long after Elk had gone his way. The diamond market was stable; the principal shares were at exactly the same figure at which they had stood for months. And the 'bears' had never really raided diamonds, though at one time they had been the most sensitive shares in the mining market.

He put through a few calls that afternoon; talked with the big City men who were vitally interested in the industry, but could gain no information that would possibly explain a fall in prices. The output was good, the world's buyers were absorbing just as many of these precious stones as came out of Africa.

Elk must have been misinformed, he decided; and in a few days the matter slipped from his mind, until . . .

He was at Ascot, walking in his garden, when he was called to the phone. He recognized the voice at the other end as one of the biggest stockbrokers in the African market.

'What's happened to de Mesnes?' he asked.

'What has happened?' asked Tony.

'They've dropped three pounds this morning and every other diamond stock is falling too. Have you heard anything of a bear raid?'

And then Tony remembered the detective's warning.

'Ask Bell and Steen,' he said, naming the firm that Elk mentioned. 'I got a tip a few days ago that they might be concerned.'

He hung up the telephone, a very thoughtful man. The fact that his own main investments were in diamond shares did not really trouble him. In the past week he had made a fortune in Lulanga Oils and there was a possibility of his making another. But why had diamonds slumped so dramatically, so unaccountably? He would have understood that phenomenon if he had known all that had been going on in a certain little Greenwich factory in the past few nights.

17

'ARE you aware,' asked Julian Reef, 'that you are being shadowed?'

Mr. Guelder started and his big mouth dropped in an expression of dismay which was comical to anybody who had not seen that expression before.

'Watched – by the police? Good Gott!' he gasped; and Julian went on with malicious satisfaction:

'I've seen Elk twice in the City lately and he was walking a few yards behind you. Do you know him?'

'The long fellow? Why, yes. He and I is friends.' In his agitation his English was not of the first quality.

'I don't know what he expects to find, but evidently he is on your trail.'

There was a pause before he put the question which was in his mind.

'Guelder, you've been going out of town a lot in the past week. I seem to remember you went to Birmingham on Monday and to Cardiff on Wednesday. What have you been doing? It seems to have irritated you.'

Rex Guelder shrugged amusedly.

'My dear fellow, I am a scientist. There are certain parts of my great machine which I must examine and test before I purchase. Wherever those parts are, there I go – it is simple.'

'Do you think Elk trailed you?'

A momentary look of alarm came to the face of the Dutchman.

'No, I should have seen him,' he said uneasily.

'Anyway, he would have found out nothing, except that you were buying electrical apparatus,' said Julian Reef, his suspicious eyes fixed on his companion.

'Zat is so,' said Mr. Guelder.

Julian, going through his correspondence a little later, found a letter addressed in a familiar hand. He tore it open, wondering what Tony Braid had to say.

It was a brief business note. In going through the share register he had noticed that certain Lulanga stock held by the dead man had not been duly transferred; or at any rate there was no record of a transfer. He enclosed the necessary documents for Julian's signature.

For a long time Reef looked at the papers, pen in hand, and then he rang for Mr. Guelder.

Mr. Guelder might know little about the mysteries of the Stock Exchange, but here was something so obvious that it was not necessary that he should be an expert in finance to appreciate it.

'How many was there?' he asked.

'About fifty thousand,' said Julian, glancing at the documents. 'To be exact, forty-nine thousand five hundred.'

He knew what the Dutchman was going to say before he spoke.

'Well, my frient! If they are not transferred they are yours, or shall I say mine? Am I not also a partner?'

Julian did not look up.

'He would not fall for that,' he said.

'But would the excellent Lady Ursula fall? She is a lady of honour,' said Guelder cunningly. 'Would she benefit by shares which are not hers?'

'They are hers all right,' said Julian roughly. 'Don't be a fool!'

'Suppose I say they do not belong to her. Suppose I go to this gentle lady mit – with a story, eh, my frient?'

Julian bit his lips. He was very badly in need of money. Not even Guelder knew how desperate was the position.

'It seems a pretty dirty trick to play,' he said lamely, at last. 'I don't like doing it, but of course they may be ours.'

Guelder patted him on the shoulder.

'Haf no fear, my frient; I will write the lady.'

Life was running with surprising smoothness at Hampstead. Ursula had a circle of friends not large but very pleasing. Though she went out very little, and scarcely entertained, she had that faculty for laying the foundations of enduring friendships which are humanity's chiefest gifts.

On the morning before diamond shares began to act so erratically, she had a letter, written in a hand which was entirely unfamiliar: it came by special messenger, and she guessed it was from a foreigner by the calligraphy, and opened it wondering who could be the person who addressed her as 'The Lady Ursula Frensham'. There were three lines of writing. To her astonishment, glancing at the signature first, she saw a flourishing scrawl which she deciphered as 'Rex Guelder'.

Lady, May I have the honour to call upon you this morning? Please see me in a matter which is most vital.

There was no address at the head of the letter and no way by which she could telephone or wire a denial of the interview.

If the truth be told, Ursula was somewhat bored that morning, or she might not have seen Mr. Guelder at all. She did not hesitate as she read the large visiting card which the maid brought to her.

'All right, ask him to come in, Minnie; and please don't allow him to stay. Come in in ten minutes on any excuse you like.'

Mr. Guelder wore a dark suit, a flaming red tie and carried a bowler hat in his hand. His golden spectacles glistened no more than his moist face, for he had walked up to Fitzjohn's Avenue, being economically minded.

'You are surprised to see me? Zat is natural. I am, as you might say, of the opposition firm! You will ask me why I did not go immediately to the excellent Mr. Braid, but in such matters as these we wish to act in the most friendly manner. It is inconceivable that I should bring you into the courts.'

He shook his head sadly at the thought.

'I am afraid I do not quite understand what it is you wish,' said Ursula. 'If it is a matter concerning Mr. Braid, I agree that it is rather useless seeing me; and if it is business then you had better see my lawyer.'

Again he shook his head.

'We want no court cases, my sweet young lady.' His eyes were devouring her, and again she had that sense of acute discomfort which she had described to Tony. 'It is the smallest matter,' he said, speaking rapidly. 'Your lamented father, whose death – ah, what tragic suddenness! – has deprived me and my dear friend Julian of a true and generous friend . . . your dear father, as I say, was associated in der business. He helt stocks, we holt stocks – whose is which? Some days I send him a few thousand, some days he sends me. We are careless men, generous, big in the heart! Yesterday morning I searched for fifty thousand shares in the Lulanga. At this surprising price who would not sell, and I a poor man? I search my safe, I ask my bank, I demand from my broker. Nothing but head-shakes. Then I search my diary, and I find fifty thousand Lulangas loaned to my lord. He had some trouble with his bank; it was needful he should put as security a hundred, two hundred – I don't know how many hundred thousand shares. He called me on the phone. "My friend Guelder, I am in a predicament. I desire to lodge shares against an overdraft, and because of the seeming worthlessness of Lulanga they demand a tremendous number." Fine! I do it in the instant! No form, no transfer, nothing. Just I send these shares by messenger-boy – remember, they are seemingly worthless, and I forgot about them. Whether the overdraft becomes accomplished or not – that is no business of mine! Who shall bother his nut about shares which are seemingly worthless? That is my predicament. It is not a matter of business, it is a matter of honour. Should I intrude upon your sorrow, I ask myself? I do not consult my good friend Julian. He also is a man of honour, very sensitive, highly principled, moreover the nephew of our dear friend Frensham. To me, of course, in strict business interests of the firm, is left the dirty work.'

He paused to take breath. Ursula had listened to the disjointed gabble, in which shrewd business was interlarded with glib sympathy, and quite understood the purport of the man's message.

'In other words, you suggest that of the two hundred thousand shares which my father left to me, fifty thousand belong to you?'

Mr. Guelder bowed.

'To my sincere regret, that is my meaning. It is deplorable, and—'

She interrupted him.

'And entirely a matter for my father's executors, is it not?' she asked.

He heaved up his shoulders deprecatingly.

'For Mr. Braid. Can I deny that – no! But if I go to Mr. Braid, what follows? He sneers, he snaps his fingers, he says "Do your damnablest." There are lawyers and processes and appearances in court and exposure of certain irregularities. For example' – he ticked off the example on one large forefinger – 'on the day of your father's death he came to the goot Julian, and demanded of him the shares which he held on your behalf. Why? For his own use. Ah, do not interrupt me. Your indignation does you honour and credit, my sweet young lady, but here is the truth, not to be denied—'

'According to Julian's own statement, those shares had been in my father's possession for some weeks,' she said coldly; and for a second Mr. Guelder was staggered.

'You desire to cover your father, but the truth must be there. We shall see on the evening newspaper proclamations "Strange Accusation Against Dead Peer". That will be unfortunate. Also at the inquest Mr. Braid swears before God that the late Frensham was not financially difficult – ah – not in financial difficulties, that is it. Was that the truth? So many things may transpire and be exposed to the low populace.'

'Mr. Guelder,' she interrupted him again, 'you are taking quite a wrong view of my position in this matter, if you imagine for one moment that I intend using the slightest influence with Mr. Braid to induce him to give you fifty thousand shares. I am not competent to deal with the matter.'

'Quite right, young lady, perfectly right,' murmured a voice, and she was so startled at the sound of it that she jumped.

Neither had heard Mr. Elk's light footstep as he crossed the lawn, nor seen his lean shadow cross the open french window.

'Never give nothing away, miss, especially when you're threatened. That's nearly blackmail.'

Guelder was glaring at him, but it was a glare of fright rather than menace.

'Mr. Elks,' he stammered, 'dis is unexpectedly a pleasure.'

'Elk,' corrected the detective. 'There's only one of us, and he's me.'

Guelder was thinking quickly. He remembered the warning that he had received from Julian Reef. He was being shadowed. And yet he had been most careful that morning. He had looked behind, he had loitered on the way, he had turned unexpectedly in search of a trailer, and there had been no sign of Elk. He was frightened, too. The laws of England were peculiarly unfair to people who deviated from the straight path of business.

'If I haf said what I should not say, most profoundly I apologize.' He made a sweeping bow to emphasize his humility.

'Most irregular and disorderly,' said Elk. He was looking at the Dutchman through half-closed eyes. 'Naturally, you're not expected to carry round a copy of *Criminal Law and Procedure*, but this is one of the countries where blackmail doesn't get past. I'm interrupting you, miss?'

She shook her head smilingly; and he might have read in her face the instant relief she felt in his presence.

'Then I must leave this matter where it is.' Guelder made a heroic effort to be detached and businesslike, which was not very successful. 'I will make formal application for restoration of the shares – I regret if I have fallen into error.'

He clicked his heels and offered a large, damp hand, first to her and then to Elk. The detective waited until the Dutchman had disappeared from view.

18

'SHARE-PUSHERS I know, but share-pullers are new ones on me. Not a friend of yours, miss?'

'He's very much not a friend of mine,' said Ursula with emphasis. 'I dislike him most intensely.'

'Woman's instinct,' murmured Elk sententiously. 'That's what I always say to the chief, "You ought to keep a woman at the Yard, just to do a little instincting – it'd save us a lot of trouble." Ever been to his house, miss?'

She shook her head.

'Queer old place, like something out of Charles Dickens. He's scientific.'

'Did you want to see me, Mr. Elk?' she asked, after a long silence.

'Well' – he hesitated – 'I did and I didn't.' He glanced round the room. 'It's a very nice house you've got, miss. It must be difficult, running a place like this. Can't think what you do when you get gentlemen up to dinner. Naturally – you can't offer 'em a cigar – that wouldn't be ladylike.'

She had heard quite a lot about Elk from Tony, and she laughed.

'I can even offer you a cigar,' she said solemnly.

She went out of the room and came back with a large box.

Mr. Elk was full of self-condemnation, but he showed the greatest care in his selection.

'Fancy me saying a thing like that! I don't know what you'll think of me. Almost like asking, isn't it? I'll take two, because I'm not sure which of these is best. I wouldn't like to take away what I might call a bad impression of your cigars. I've got a nasty job this morning. That's the worst of the Yard, they won't leave you to work out a really interesting crime, but push you off on twiddling little affairs that a flat-footed policeman could do twice as well. God forgive me for speaking disrespectfully of the uniformed branch – I was one myself.'

'What interesting crime are you on now?'

He was cutting the end of the cigar with a huge clasp-knife and he did not look up for some few seconds.

'That Guelder's a crime in himself,' he said. 'He's an offence against the law of nature. I don't know that I've ever seen a worse crime than him.'

She was amused.

'Are you very much concerned with Mr. Guelder?'

'In a way – only in a way, miss.'

And then he changed the subject and told her of his new case.

The police had found at Plumstead, which is near Woolwich, a small detached villa, occupied by one who was apparently a middle-aged clerk and his wife, a stoutish gentleman who went into Woolwich to business every morning with great punctuality and dug up his garden on Saturday afternoon. That he did not go to church on Sunday was not counted against him, because so few people did.

'And he is nearly the biggest receiver south of the Thames – we found him by accident. They say that villa's chock-full of property, from diamond rings to tapestries – one of the men at the Yard told me there's nearly a quarter of a million pounds' worth of goods there. The chap bought everything that came to him. He's going to be difficult to convict because he carried on a genuine business as a dealer; and he's got a big store in Woolwich, where he bought and sold freely. They say he would buy a barge-load if it brought the right stuff. All the river hooks came to him: nothing was too big, nothing too small. I'm not really in the case,' he explained. 'I'm exercising a supervision, which means I'll get all the credit if there's any going, and the fellow under me will get all the kicks if any are due.'

'Has it anything to do with Mr. Guelder?'

'Him? Good Lord, no!' said Elk, with a contempt he did not try to disguise. 'This receiver feller is *clever!*'

19

GUELDER found a cab at the top of Hill Street, and indulged in an unusual luxury. He was still agitated and breathless when he came to the office. Julian was out, but came in a few minutes later to find his friend in a very perturbed condition of mind.

'She would give nothing,' he said.

Julian guffawed.

'Did you imagine she would, you poor simpleton? I knew that little scheme of yours was a failure before you started. I was hoping you had the brains to keep me out of it.'

'I have brains in plenty,' snarled the other. 'Did you say this before I went? Did you not say that this was a good scheme? – Elk was there.'

'Elk?' Julian frowned. 'He trailed you?'

'Whether he trailed or whether he snailed I do not know,' said the Dutchman savagely. 'He was there! He comes in at a moment when I perhaps would have convinced her. Even now that money would come if you would take action through your lawyers . . .'

'I don't think it is necessary,' said Julian, to his surprise. 'I've been having a meeting with the people I suggested we should let in on our scheme, and they will find all the money we want.'

Guelder's face brightened.

'They are a little sceptical about your invention and two or three of them are coming tonight to see a demonstration. Show me that stone again.'

Guelder unlocked the safe, took out a small jeweller's case, opened it, and placed it on the table. Inside, a small pure white diamond sent multi-coloured rays with every movement of the case.

'How long did this take?'

'Three hours,' said Guelder promptly. 'In time it shall be done more quickly, but even that acceleration is quite unnecessary. It needs only, my dear Julian, the duplication of instruments, and increased power of light, an added efficiency of apparatus.'

'They're coming in this morning to see it,' said Julian, 'and if they're satisfied, they're beginning operations on the market this afternoon, even before they have seen the experiment with their own eyes. I have told them that you would treat an even bigger stone.'

Guelder nodded.

'Exactly! Tonight I will experiment with a large cushion-shape of ten carats. That indeed will be something worth seeing!'

He was curious to discover why these usually cautious City men would begin their manipulations of stock before they were convinced as to the value of his experiment.

'The market is weak, especially the diamond market,' explained Julian. 'There have been a number of independent little alluvial fields opened up in Africa and the big companies are working for legislation to limit the output. They think the diamond market is so weak that even without this discovery of yours they could safely raid it.'

He told Guelder what the Dutchman did not know – he only took a very scrappy interest in mining affairs – that there was an intense rivalry between a small group of millionaires who had been 'squeezed out' of the diamond industry by a bigger group, and were keen to deal the industry a staggering blow.

There were one or two serious matters on which Julian would have liked to speak and which, but for that unnerving exchange he had had with Guelder, would have been the subject of a sharp rebuke. Guelder was extravagant: he knew nothing of the value of money. It was his habit to buy imperially in the pursuit of his profitable hobby and to leave his partner to foot the bill. A number of very heavy accounts had come in that morning, one of which, considerably over two thousand pounds, had demanded instant payment.

He did mildly remonstrate.

'In a week or two's time it won't matter, but just now we've got to be very careful. I am staking a great deal on your scheme and I want to see my way out if it should go wrong.'

Guelder smiled slowly.

'There is no way out, my friend,' he said, in his quietest tone. 'We are committed completely – to the extent of your business and beyond! I will give you a word of advice, my dear Julian. Money is a definite thing. It matters nothing whence it comes. You may win a fortune by my discovery, you may also win a fortune by its promise.'

'I don't know what you mean,' said Julian, frowning.

Guelder grinned.

'Your friends are going to "bear" the market – goot! Does it matter whether you win money by the "bearing" of the market or by my discovery, whether you win money by persuading our Twister to give you fifty thousand shares or by digging a hole in the ground and finding a gold reef? Be sensible and intelligent, my frient. The race is nothing; the goal, the winning tape, the reward, is all!'

Julian Reef was a little bewildered, but forbore to ask any further questions. Half an hour later came three soberly dressed City men who moved in no atmosphere of romance, and brought with them none of the glamour of adventure; yet in their intent were pirates and treasure-seekers and assassins all in one.

Mr. Elk's duties took him into queer places, some pleasant, some squalid. His visit to Woolwich produced both experiences. The villa at Plumstead, which he had described as 'little', was in point of fact a dwelling of some pretensions. It boasted a garage and extensive underground cellars. There was no disorder here; if the articles which went to its embellishment had been stolen they had been effectively utilized.

Mr. Weldin, the owner, had not stored his stolen pictures in the cellar; that was the place for wine. Rare wines there were, in enormous quantities. A certain old master which had been cut from its frame in the Louvre was re-framed and hanging in his bedroom and it was this, curiously enough, which had been his undoing, for there had been a leaky pipe in Mr. Weldin's bathroom and a plumber had been summoned to deal with this commonplace domestic tragedy. He was specially privileged, because nobody was ever admitted to the house; Mrs. Weldin did the housework herself.

It was bad luck for this prince of receivers that the plumber had artistic leanings, and in his spare time attended painting classes. The last person in the world one would have expected to recognize instantly a stolen Corot was a journeyman plumber. Not only did he know its origin and history, but he knew all the circumstances of its theft.

He left the house, having done his duty as a plumber; and proceeded to the police station, where he did his duty as an artist and a citizen.

'Doesn't seem natural to me,' said Elk. 'I thought these trade unions kept painting and plumbing distinct.'

He was being shown round the beautiful residence preparatory to his visit to the more squalid scene of Mr. Weldin's minor activities. This was a riverside warehouse, stacked with a nondescript collection of articles, from old clothing hanging precisely upon hooks, to unopened bales of merchandise that had been lifted by the river pirates.

'A lot of the stuff has been genuinely bought and paid for; a lot has undoubtedly come into his possession illegally,' said the local inspector, who was a precise man with an official vocabulary. 'As a matter of fact, he's got receipts for a good many of the big things in his house – the pictures, for instance. Weldin says he didn't know the value of the Corot.'

'What's that?' asked the puzzled Elk. 'Oh, the picture! Is that how you pronounce it? What a marvellous thing is education, Inspector! If you take my advice, you'll examine all this junk very carefully – particularly the clothing. Very likely you'll get a bigger charge against him if you do. Maybe you'll be doing him a favour if you only charge him with robbery.'

He interviewed Mr. Weldin in his cell and found him very cheerful and confident.

'There never was such an outrage committed upon a citizen and a taxpayer,' he began, but Elk stopped him gently.

'That line of talk was fine before they invented finger-prints, Weldin; and we've just had your record back from the Yard, Weldin, Martin, Cootes, Colonel Slane, John B. Sennet, or whatever your real name is.'

Weldin laughed, for he had a sense of humour.

'If ever you meet the man who invented finger-prints, will you give him a slug on the head for me, Elk?'

'I'll think about it,' said Mr. Elk genially, and left the stout robber to his fate.

'I'm going to do a bit of investigating,' he told his clerk, 'and I'm not to be disturbed.'

'What time would you like to be awakened, sir?' asked the clerk, without any offensive intent.

'With a cup of tea at five,' said Elk, and within a few minutes of turning the key in the lock was taking his afternoon nap.

The evening brought a summons to Woolwich and he went without complaint. He noticed on a newspaper bill something about 'Diamond Slump', but that did not interest him, though the news back of the bill had been sufficient to bring Tony Braid back to London in a hurry.

Tony called at various houses in Mayfair, discussed in quiet studies the meaning of the drop and found that one at least of the diamond millionaires had an explanation for the slump.

'Sleser's in the market,' said one, a good-looking, grey-bearded man identified with the industry. 'He may or may not burn his fingers, but certainly we're not going to spend money to fight him. Our shares are worth just what they were quoted before the drop, and they will return to normal in the natural course. There isn't anything to be scared about.'

Tony smiled.

'Personally, I'm not very scared,' he said. 'Only I'm wondering whether Reef is behind it.'

'Reef?' The bearded man frowned. 'Who the devil is Reef?'

If Julian had heard him he would have hated him.

'Oh yes, I remember! But why should he be "bearing"

diamonds? Anyway, we're doing nothing, and the only advice I can give you—'

'Is quite unnecessary,' laughed Tony. 'If the slump continues I'm a buyer, though my buying will not greatly affect the price.'

Other men did not take the same philosophical view. Already they had tables showing the enormous depreciation of capital value and they were inclined to be alarmed at the prospect of a further fall. Each named a different man as being behind the bear raid, but all mentioned Sleser – the millionaire who hated the diamond group worse than he hated exercise. It was clear to Tony that the attack upon diamonds was a much more extensive and serious affair than he had at first thought.

From one man on whom he called he heard an extraordinary story. The brother of the chauffeur lived at Greenwich and he had heard that there was a riverside factory which was engaged in manufacturing diamonds by artificial means!

'Which, of course, is punk!' said Tony. 'It's quite possible to make diamonds, but they are so minute that they have no commercial value; and the cost of production entirely puts them out of the competitive field.'

Yet he was intrigued . . . Greenwich!

Guelder lived at Greenwich and, as he had heard, owned a small factory. The man was a scientist, brilliant, by all accounts. Was it then true that Julian was behind the slump? He had no illusions about Julian's importance; he was a struggler who made an impressive show but was, he knew, without any strong financial backing. Julian lived from hand to mouth; in some years he had made enormous sums of money, in other years – and this was not so widely advertised – had lost even larger sums – but he was without sound or stable foundation. Tony had done his best, by hints and suggestions, to convey this fact to the young man's uncle, but Frensham suffered from an exaggerated sense of loyalty and had, too, a genuine faith in the ability of the younger man.

20

AT nine o'clock that night, when Tony was debating whether he should go to his club, where he knew he would find one or two men interested in the latest market development, or whether he should return to Ascot, the telephone bell rang. His man did not answer the ring. He was rather inefficient and was sulking under notice to leave. Tony went to the instrument, and after a little while he heard Elk's voice.

'I've been ringing you up in the country – it cost me ninepence. When I say "me" I mean the Government. I want you to come down here.'

'Where are you?' asked Tony.

'At Woolwich.' He gave the address. 'And, Mr. Braid, do you think you could bring along the young lady?'

'Lady Ursula Frensham?' asked Tony, in surprise.

'Yes. I want her more than you.'

'What is the idea?'

He was evidently considering how he should reply.

'It's a matter of identification. A coat that's been found. I wouldn't trouble you, but it's rather important.'

'But how on earth can she identify a coat?'

'I'll tell you when you come. The local inspector got on to Reef, but happily for all concerned he was out. Will you bring her down?'

'Certainly, if it's necessary, and if I can get her.'

'And, Mr. Braid, it's raining down here, so don't come in your convertible. I'm hoping you'll be able to give me a lift back to Town, and I hate the cold. If you'd bring the Rolls – that big red one – I'd be obliged. You used to keep a silver cigar-box under the seat?'

'I will bring the Rolls and the cigar-box – and I will see that the cigar-box is filled, you old mendicant!'

'How's that, Mr. Braid?' asked Elk's anxious voice. 'Mendi-something? Oh, I get you! The Coronas – if they're too big to go in the box you might put 'em in the boot.'

As soon as he had rung off, Tony got on to Ursula and told her what had happened.

'Why he wants you, heaven knows, but he's very serious about it. Do you feel like taking a flight into the wilds of Woolwich?'

'I'd love it,' she said. 'I'll come down in my car—'

'I'll come up in mine,' said Tony. 'Elk particularly asked for the Rolls.'

She was waiting for him when he arrived. The rain at Woolwich had reached the west of London by the time he had picked her up, and most of the way they drove through a blinding storm which reached its zenith by the time they reached Blackheath.

She had not seen him since Guelder's call, and she was able to give him a full account of what had passed. To her surprise, Tony did not scoff at the story which the Dutchman had put forward.

'That sort of thing, the exchanging of shares, must have been going on all the time,' he said. 'I'm afraid that your father was the most unbusinesslike man that ever undertook to run a company! If it came to law, we might have a very big difficulty in proving that your two hundred thousand shares do not belong to somebody else! The transfer books were vilely kept; and to my knowledge big bunches of stock were still in Reef's name. As a matter of fact, I am responsible for this demand. I found a number of shares hadn't been duly transferred and sent the papers to Julian. From this the great scheme must have been born.'

'It terrifies me, Tony . . . no, no, not Julian. I feel so contemptuous of him that he somehow doesn't count, it's Guelder! I can't describe to you how vile he is – it's not his words or actions, it's his eyes.'

He felt her shiver, sought and found her hand in the dark.

'Greenwich will be in mourning for Guelder if he comes to see you again,' he said. 'I think I'll have a little private talk with him.'

'It's stupid of me,' she protested. 'You have met men like Guelder before.'

He had to open the window that separated them from the chauffeur and give him the direction when they reached Woolwich, for although Elk had been explicit in his directions, it was some little time before they passed into the silent street where the warehouse was situated.

Elk, sheltered from the rain, was waiting in the doorway by the side of a policeman in shining oilskins.

'Sorry to bring you down here, Lady Ursula, especially on a low receiving case. Has that bargeman arrived?' He addressed the question to somebody invisible in the darkness, and a voice answered in the affirmative. 'This way, Lady Ursula – mind the step.'

He flashed a light before them and they passed down a short passage which smelt damp and unpleasant. At the end of the passage was a door, which he opened. Ursula found herself in a room illuminated by a very dim light hanging from the raftered ceiling and affording just enough light to reveal the hopeless confusion of the place. There were shelves and racks covered with shadowy packages; huge canvas-covered bales littered the floor. Even the dusky rafters were hung with shapeless bundles.

'Mind how you walk.' Elk took her arm and guided her between the impedimenta into a small office at the farther end of the room. Here the lighting was more adequate.

An old roll-top desk, a table and a chair comprised the furniture. There was a year-old calendar hanging on the wall, attached to which were a few dusty shelves covered with torn papers and ancient office books.

On the table was spread a dark overcoat; and Tony knew that it was the garment which had brought them to Woolwich.

'I'm not going to tell you a long yarn about this man Weldin,' said Elk. 'Anyway, it's not my story, but Inspector Frame's.' He nodded to the tall, good-looking man who had followed them into the office. 'Frame's in charge of the case. Now this is the tale I'm going to tell you. We found the coat – or rather the inspector did – amongst others, and we searched it to see if there was any chance of finding the owner. We found the owner first pop: his name is written on the inside of the pocket by the tailor, and he is a mutual friend of ours.'

'I think I know who it is,' said Tony.

'We'll come to that,' said Elk. 'We put an inquiry through to the gentleman—'

'Julian Reef?'

'Mr. Julian Reef. He wasn't in. Then we found that the coat had been honestly bought by Weldin and sold by the honest seaman outside. There was a record of it in Weldin's books. Now bring in that bargeman.'

Inspector Frame disappeared and came back accompanied by a tall, thick-set man with a weather-beaten face and a mop of grey hair, who seemed a little terrified by the sense that in some vague way he was associated with wrong-doing.

'Now what's your yarn, mister?' asked Elk.

'What I told you before, sir,' said the bargeman, in a deep, gruff voice. 'A week or so ago I was coming down the river at the tiller of my barge. She was empty – *Polly Ann* her name is – having been up to Kingston to take a cargo of bricks. We were being towed down the river by a tug and I was at the helm, half asleep I'll admit, because I'd only had four hours' sleep the night before. The tug-master sounded his siren just before we went under Westminster Bridge – I think there was a boat in the way – and that woke me up, though I could have slept without any danger, because we were lashed to another barge. We passed under the bridge and just as we were clear, something fell over my head. It gave me a rare start. I thought my mate was having a lark with me. When I pulled it off there was nobody in sight except the man at the tiller of the other barge, and I decided that somebody must have dropped it from Westminster Bridge. It was that coat. I didn't know what to do with it; I'm too big a man to wear a thing like that, so after keeping it in my cabin for a trip I sold it to Zonnerheim's in Artillery Street—'

'That's another name for Weldin. He had lots of collecting places,' explained Elk to Tony. And then, to the bargeman: 'Thank you, Mr. What's-your-name. The police accept your story. Mr. Frame has got your address if he wants you.'

The man seemed very thankful to be released from his embarrassing obligation.

'It's a very interesting story,' said Tony; 'but I don't quite see why you brought us down, Elk. I'm not in a position to identify Julian Reef's clothing, and I'm perfectly certain that Lady Ursula isn't.'

But apparently she was.

'Yes, I know the coat. I've seen Julian wearing it,' she said and picked it up.

It was of dark-blue serge, very light of weight and the lining was of silk; it was, to Tony's experienced eye, almost new.

'Show 'em the paper, Frame,' said Elk.

Inspector Frame took a sheet of thin paper from his pocket and spread it out on the table. It had evidently been badly crumpled; rolled into a ball, Tony guessed. There was a line and a half of writing.

'Read it,' said Elk; and, bending over, Tony read:

For years I have been engaged in foolish speculation. I confess . . .

Tony frowned. The words seemed familiar.

'Well?' said Elk, watching his face.

'May I see it?' asked Ursula.

Elk handed the paper to her; and Anthony saw her mouth open in amazement.

'Why, this is the—' She did not finish what she had to say, but looked from one to the other in amazement.

'That's right,' nodded Elk.

'It is what Father wrote before – before—'

Then in a flash Tony remembered. The words were identical with those which had been found by the side of Frensham's dead body.

'Do you recognize the handwriting, Lady Ursula?'

She was silent. Too well she knew that writing.

'Do you recognize it?'

Her lips trembled.

'I don't know . . . I shouldn't like to say. What does it mean? Will you tell me just what depends upon my identifying this writing?'

'Not much,' said Elk, to her infinite relief. 'There are scores of other people who could recognize it. Do you know it, Mr. Braid?'

Tony read it again.

'Yes,' he said quietly. 'It is Julian Reef's.'

Again Elk nodded.

'That's what I thought. Queer, the first lines of the confession . . . same words as Frensham wrote, but in a different hand. What do you make of that, Mr. Braid?'

Tony shook his head.

'I can make nothing of it,' he said. 'It is staggering.'

'It doesn't stagger me any,' said Elk. He took the paper, folded it and put it in his pocket. 'I'll keep this for the Yard. We're very fond of curios there . . . Exhibit A. I'll give you a receipt for it, Inspector. It doesn't really belong to this case, but to another. And I'll keep the coat, which is pretty important. I want a sheet of paper to wrap it.'

Elk sat by the chauffeur on the way back to town; the open glass partition brought him into the party, he said.

'Life's full of coincidences,' he mused, puffing luxuriously at the long cigar which he had accepted as his due. 'If you put these things in a book, nobody would believe 'em. The Weldin case is a big one, but it's got nothing to do with the late Lord Frensham; and here we've picked up a Fact that has got a lot to do with him. Here's a bargee sitting at home in the bosom of his family and telling his fat wife – I'll bet she's fat – of the awful time the police have been giving him about an old coat. If he hadn't been at Kingston delivering bricks, that coat wouldn't have been in this car.'

'What does it signify . . . the coat and this paper? I – I don't understand it.'

Elk was uncommunicative.

'Everything means something,' he said tritely. And, to Tony: 'You don't mind going back through Greenwich? It's not the best road by a long chalk, but I've got an idea. How would you like to be a detective, Lady Ursula?'

'I should hate it,' she said frankly.

The reply afforded Mr. Elk a great deal of amusement, and he chuckled for a long time.

'Would you like to be one tonight? I thought of just giving the once-over to that Dutchman's family mansion.'

'Does he live at Greenwich?' she asked.

'He does, and Greenwich is a very nice place,' said Elk, surprisingly. 'I was born there. I was the only man ever born in Greenwich, as far as I know. At least, I've never met anybody else.'

Every now and again he gave a new instruction to the driver. They had left the main road and were threading a way through a labyrinth of small streets and always bearing to the right.

'That's the river.' Elk pointed between two tall buildings. Somewhere in the rain a red light glowed.

'Ship,' said Elk, briefly. 'He's anchoring there, waiting for the tide. They've got to be careful of the top of Millwall Tunnel.'

Now they were taking rather a wide detour and were back in the main road again. Tony wondered why the detective had left him, but Elk offered no explanation. He did those kinds of senseless things which had not only apparently but absolutely no reason.

He was intensely curious, he confessed, and liked visiting familiar places. Later, Tony learnt that the detective had deviated for purely sentimental reasons – he wished to pass the house in which he was born and which he had not seen for thirty-five years.

21

THEY left behind the great grey palace, where kings had died, and again plunged into a wilderness of little streets, until they came to a crooked and deserted thoroughfare, so narrow that two cars would have found it difficult to pass.

'We'll stop here,' said Elk. 'The other chauffeurs will think we're one of the gang.'

Tony leaned forward and peered through the rain-blurred windscreen. There were undoubtedly other cars in the street – big ones, judging by the headlights.

'Guelder's giving a party,' suggested Elk. 'Do you mind waiting here?'

He got out of the car and disappeared into the night.

'I think that is the house and the factory on the right,' said Tony, letting down a window.

Ursula looked and shivered.

'Horrible, isn't it? There's a menace about this place which makes me go cold. It's so sinister, so macabre. Why on earth does he live here?'

'Because he's sinister and macabre,' said Tony.

She thought he was going to get out and clutched his arm. 'Don't leave me, please. Look at that little doorway . . . like some horrible old prison. There are no windows and that street lamp on a wall bracket is like something out of a picture of Old London. Ugh!'

'I have no doubt it has a beauty in Guelder's eyes,' said Tony. 'In fact, it's rather picturesque by daylight.'

Tony had seen some figures moving in the light of a street lamp and he put his head out of the car window. They were chauffeurs, as the keen-eyed Elk had seen. He spoke to his own chauffeur in a low tone and the man got out and drifted away.

'I want to know who these visitors are,' he said. 'There is a certain freemasonry among car-drivers, and I dare say he'll be more informative than Elk.'

It was the detective who returned first.

'Can't quite make it out,' he said. 'This fellow Guelder's giving some sort of lecture to the alight – élite, is it? Where's your chauffeur?'

'I sent him to find out who these car-owners were.'

'Good!' said Elk. 'I didn't want to ask, but these fellows are talkative. There are some big people in Greenwich tonight – I saw two big cars in the street, besides ours.'

The chauffeur returned soon afterwards and was very informative.

'Mostly gentlemen from the City,' he reported. 'One is Mr. Sleser – they say he's a millionaire—'

'Sleser?' said Tony quickly, and remembered his bearded friend's suggestion. 'Who else?'

The chauffeur told him two names which were familiar to him, but men who operated indiscriminately in all markets; they were the supreme gamblers of the City and were prepared to take a flutter in mines or provisions or rubber, as opportunity arose.

'Did they ask you who you were?' demanded Tony, and the chauffeur grinned.

'I said I was a hired car that had brought a gentleman from Grosvenor Place,' he said, and was commended for his unveracity.

The car had to be backed from the narrow street. Not until they had struck the brightly illuminated main road did Ursula breathe freely.

'I was terrified,' she said. 'Isn't that childish of me? And I'm not usually like that, Tony. Why did these important people come in their cars to Guelder's house?'

'I'd give a lot to know. You didn't by any chance find your way into Guelder's place, did you, Elk?'

Elk had not, though he had tried.

'I knocked at the door, and an old lady came – must have been about a hundred years old: possibly more; and she couldn't speak English. I know six sentences in French and I tried 'em all, but she's German, I guess – or Dutch. The door was on the chain, too, all the time she was talking. There was a nice smell of cooking: I guess they're stopping to supper. It was pretty tough on me, the only genuine starving man in London. If you ask me to supper after that, Mr. Braid, I'll never forgive myself. I'm always giving people the impression that I'm a moocher and I'm the most generous man in the world. I've given more folks away than anybody I know. But if you did ask me to supper – and I'd die of shame if you as much as mentioned it – what's the matter with Kirro's? You needn't dress if you feed on the balcony, and you can get a drink up till one.'

'Kirro's it shall be,' said Tony, 'unless you'd rather come back to my house.'

'I don't like your cooking,' said Elk, calmly. 'Now if you don't mind, I'd like you to drop me at the Yard and I'll join you a quarter of an hour afterwards – I want to put these parcels some place where they won't be mishandled.'

Accordingly, Elk was set down at the gloomy entrance of Scotland Yard, and within a stone's throw of the spot where a light summer overcoat had dropped fluttering over the parapet to envelop the head of an astonished bargee.

Although the floor of Kirro's club was gay and lively with dancers, the balcony was practically deserted.

'An astonishing man, Elk,' said Tony, thoughtfully. 'You never know what's going on in his mind, although he is apparently the most transparent creature.'

'I'm really worried about the paper and the coat,' said the girl. 'I feel there is going to be bad trouble – and in some way I shall be affected.'

She had been very silent all the way from Woolwich, and had scarcely spoken at all since they had left the front of Guelder's house.

'It gives me such a – an ugly feeling, Tony. Have you any idea what is behind it?'

'If I had, I shouldn't tell you,' he said.

He was looking at her anxiously; she was paler than he remembered seeing her. He told her so.

'Don't be silly, it's nothing, unless it was that horrible place at Greenwich. You know the expression, "walking over your own grave"? That's just how I felt in that horrid street. And it wasn't hysteria. Mr. Elk says I have an instinct and I think, with any encouragement, he would have recommended me for a job at Scotland Yard!'

'Has Guelder been unpleasant to you? I wish you'd tell me. Ursula.'

She shook her head.

'No, he hasn't. And yet, Tony . . . as I sat in the car in that street I found myself wishing he were dead! Isn't that ghastly? I never felt that way towards any man, and I have no reason at all. Of course, he's fearfully affectionate and friendly, but then so many European men are. But I've just got that feeling that he'll do me some terrible injury, and every time I see his round, foolish face I want to hit him!'

She was breathless. He had never seen her like that before, so tense, so vehement. He judged she was still suffering from the reaction of her father's death, and was perhaps a little over-tired, and he humoured her.

'You must get Elk to report him. I'm sure he could trace up some crime—'

'Ask Mr. Elk yourself,' she said, looking over his shoulder at the lank figure of the detective.

121

'Ask him what?' said Elk, as he sat down, and she gasped.
'You didn't hear me?'

'Read your lips – it's easy when you know how. See that fellow down there?' He pointed to a florid man who was sitting with a very pretty girl at one of the tables, leaning slightly towards her. 'Do you know what he's saying? Give you three guesses.'

'Something very affectionate, I'm sure,' said Ursula.

'He's talking about cream – shoe-cream,' said Elk, watching the unconscious man closely. 'I got him now – he's telling her how he gets shoe-cream for his hunting-boots.'

'Not really?' said Ursula.

Elk nodded.

'There's one thing about life you've got to learn, young lady – that people are always saying the thing you don't expect! You were easier, because you move your mouth. Most ladies nowadays talk through their noses, and I'm no nose-reader. What was it you were going to ask me?'

'Whether you would deport Guelder,' said Tony.

'He's the one man I'll never deport,' said the detective, with emphasis. 'No, I like old Guelder – like to have him round. I'll get him a nice home one of these days, but bless you, they treat these fellows so well in prison that they're better off.'

'Mr. Elk,' said Ursula, lowering her voice, 'what is the meaning of the paper you found in Julian's overcoat? Have you any idea?'

'Means quite a lot to me,' said Elk. 'It's plainer than that – than that bow-legged boy that's dancing with the beautiful girl down there. I know her: her father was a bookmaker and a sinner. Plain to you, too, isn't it, Mr. Braid?'

Tony hesitated.

'No,' he said, at last. 'I have decided that I don't wish it to be too plain to me.'

'I think you're wise,' murmured Elk.

The waiter had approached, and was standing expectantly by.

'Welsh rarebit,' said Elk in an undertone, 'with a large egg on top. Don't offer me champagne, or I'll drink it. My doctor told me it was good for me, but it must be very dry. I suppose you've never met a fellow like me, Lady Ursula? Do you know what they used to call me in the H Division? – Cadging Cuthbert – and the curious thing is my name's not Cuthbert at all.'

Then of a sudden the drawl dropped from his voice.

'Want to know all about that little bit of paper? Well, I can't tell you, miss. A police officer can pull your leg up to a certain point, but beyond that it's against the rules. I want about three other pieces of evidence before I can talk to you and then I doubt if I will. You'll have to get it out of the papers.'

He changed the subject with a brusqueness foreign to him; and very wisely Tony did not attempt to re-open it.

They left the club at half-past twelve. The rain was still pelting down. The linkman who was usually at the door with an umbrella to protect the departing guests had gone to fetch a cab for another member.

'We'll walk to the parking place,' suggested Tony, and helped the girl into her coat.

To reach the quiet square where the cars were parked they took a short cut which brought them through a narrow street which was bisected by one even more narrow. A motorist had stopped his car in such a position that it was athwart the thoroughfare down which they were walking. They heard the hum and purr of the engine before they discerned the dim shape of the car.

'It seems to me,' Elk was saying, 'that that's a dangerous place to stop—'

Plop! Plop!

They saw two quick stabs of flame from the interior of the car, something whanged past Elk's left ear and he heard the smack of a bullet as it struck a projecting sign-board.

'Doghound!' roared Elk, and leapt forward like a sprinter at the crack of the starter's pistol.

Before he was half-way to his objective the car had moved on, faster and faster; he saw not even the faint tail-light of it as it disappeared.

'Me or you?' said Elk. 'That's the only question I've got to decide. If it was you, I know the man; but if it was intended for me, it might be one of six!'

22

JULIAN had accompanied his partner back to Greenwich that night and travelled with him by bus, a type of vehicle which the red-haired man loathed beyond all others.

'Economy in little things, my frient,' said Guelder, 'is the foundation of fortune! The next time you come to me it shall be in a gilded chariot, drawn by white horses mit gold hoofs! But now der bus is the best.'

'I suppose those people will find their way tonight?' asked Julian. 'I don't suppose any of them know where Greenwich is?'

Mr. Guelder did not share his doubts.

'I haf given them all the plans wit' express instructions. Tonight we will have a grand party in my little house, eh? Freda will be enraged; already she has told me she will go back to Holland if I have visitors. Freda is amusement for me!'

'Why do you live so far out of town?' asked Julian, not for the first time.

'I like the sea air that comes up the river. Also I was born on the top of water. In my part of Holland you cannot walk for fife minutes without falling into a canal or into a dyke – I like the smell of water, the big ships that come up and down, and the little boats I see – at night! I watch them from my window all through the night sometimes; I see them slinking along the shore, like rats – water-rats; and I have heard and seen things in dose dark hours, my frient, dat would make your poor blood turn to ice!'

It had not this effect upon Mr. Rex Guelder, if his delighted smile meant anything.

'So you see, Greenwich is desirable to me. Also, my frient, on a foggy night, could you not imagine how simple it would be for a poor hunted Hollander who was wanted by the police – supposing that disaster – to slip down on the long highway that leads to all the worlt? No ports, no Customs, no prying police officer lookint into the faces of passengers as they go on the boat, no passport – just you and the sea and the fog!'

Julian shivered.

'Darned uncomfortable I call that.'

Rex Guelder smiled again.

'To me a joy,' he said.

'I suppose if anything went wrong you would go back to Holland?'

He heard the man grunt.

'Dat is not my country no more,' he said, emphatically.

Freda, so far from proving at all difficult, gave Julian almost an enthusiastic welcome. Her English was poor. She began a sentence correctly enough, and then seemed to lose courage and tail off into an incoherent jumble of sound which even Guelder could not interpret. A wonderful woman, he called her in her absence.

Julian, who had never been to the living part of Guelder's house, was astonished at the neatness and the cleanness of everything: there was not a piece of brass that did not pay testimony to the old woman's industry. He made acquaintance, too, with the three guardian angels of the establishment. They sat side by side, as though they had been trained to the position – three big white cats with green eyes, the biggest cats that Julian had ever seen.

For half an hour, while dinner was being prepared, they sat on the window-seat, watching the traffic pass up and down the Thames in the dusk of the evening. Guelder broke the silence as he lit a new and even viler cigar than he had been smoking.

'I wish very much we could fix dat man Braid,' he said. 'My frient, there was a time when you would have a clever little spy in his house. I remember when you had that trouble with Crostuck and how useful it was to know from the maid that Mr. Crostuck was going abroad, eh?'

Julian threw the end of his cigarette through the window and watched it fall through the rotting planks of the wharf into the mud below.

'It would be quite useless so far as Braid is concerned,' he said. 'I put in a man a month ago. It cost me a tenner to place him, and he hasn't been worth it. Unfortunately, Braid doesn't take him to Ascot, and that, of course, limits his usefulness. Up to now he's told me very little. What's more, Braid is getting a little suspicious of him.'

The other looked at him admiringly.

'The so clever Julian!' he chuckled.

'He's a dull dog, and not too well blessed with grey matter. He has excellent facilities, too.' Julian went on. 'Braid has a telephone extension in his bedroom; it is quite possible to pick up the receiver in the bedroom and hear all that Braid is saying on the dining-room telephone.'

He looked at his watch impatiently, and at that moment Freda came in with the dinner. It was quite dark by the time the first of the visitors arrived, and was shown into the big sitting-room. The second and third came immediately on his heels, but they had to wait some time before the fourth and the fifth arrived together. They were a cheerfully sceptical lot of hard-headed men; and yet when they came to discuss the experiment to be witnessed, not one of them could deny its possibility.

'I've often thought it was possible,' said Sleser, the thick bull-necked millionaire. 'I know you can take white diamonds and turn them pink by the application of X-rays, and I've always thought it must be feasible to take yellow diamonds which isn't worth a tenth of the value of a blue-white, and get the amber out of it.'

Rex Guelder beamed complacently upon the speaker.

'It is not only possible,' he said, 'but it is accomplished!'

'What will this mean to you apart from what you make out of the market?' asked another of Julian.

'Immediately? I've fifteen thousand pounds' worth of coloured stones in this safe, collected from all over Europe,' said Julian. 'I rather fancy we paid much more for many of them than they were worth, but not a quarter of their value when we turn them white.'

'And you can do this?' asked Sleser, his dull eyes questioning the Dutchman.

'It is done,' said Guelder with a smirk. 'Tonight you will see the process.'

Sleser grunted something, and humped himself into a more comfortable position.

'This process will revolutionize the market,' he said. 'It will simply mean that thousands of stones which have been and will be cut and sold for practically a song will come into competition with whites. Your fifteen thousand pounds' worth of stones may be worth a hundred thousand. What is more important is that thousands upon thousands of stones which are now rejected and sold as faults will be available for the market: it is a curious fact that some of the biggest diamonds have found a tint.'

He puffed at his cigar a little longer, his eyes fixed on the carpet.

'The market is bound to panic as soon as this is known. There must be hundreds and thousands of yellow diamonds in the world that will be worth as much as the best blue-white that was ever found at Kimberley. I've been working it out and I've reached the conclusion that the least we can expect is a fifty per cent drop in all the leading diamond shares. Shut that door, Reef, and tell that old woman not to come in until we have finished our chat.'

'She won't come in,' said Guelder promptly, 'and she cannot speak English.'

'What I propose,' said Sleser, 'is this. If the experiment satisfies me and satisfies our friends here, we will go to work at once and form a little company, which we will call the Coloration Syndicate. The chief value will be to advertise the fact that we have faith in the new method. I take it we'll all subscribe to that flotation. The capital need not be large. We will take over the process, open a factory somewhere on the South Coast, and take in a few titled directors to give it tone. In the meantime, and tomorrow morning, we go after de Mesne shares and punch 'em right down into the ground! Tomorrow noon we'll issue a statement to the Press containing particulars of the invention. You'd better fix up to have the stones photographed so that we can send the copies to the Press. Next day we'll give particulars of the new company. By then, I should imagine, diamond shares will be at such a price that we'll be able to cover and make a pretty big profit.'

He rose, dusted some cigar-ash off his knee.

'Now let us see this marvellous plant of yours, Guelder. I'm beginning to believe it is a fake – or that I'm dreaming.'

23

GUELDER led the way through the iron door to the bench at the farther end of the room. He had had six chairs placed for his audience. He passed from hand to hand a square-cut diamond which was so deep a yellow that it was almost brown.

'This is the stone, gentlemens, with which I experiment. It is of great value and the largest stone I have yet used; I chose this because of its peculiar shape, and because I think that its particular refractive qualities may give me better results in a stone of this shape.'

He turned over his switches and laid the stone in the agate depression. They crowded round, watching, until there was a blinding flash and a crackle of blue sparks leapt from the machine in the direction of the spectators.

'Please it is nothing,' said Guelder, as they shrank back.

He took from a teacup a spoonful of white dust, and poured it over the diamond on the agate until it was invisible, before he submitted the heap of white dust to the electrical bombardment.

'What is the blue light?' somebody asked, and Guelder launched forth into a long technical explanation, which was gibberish to most of the people there.

Forming part of the instrument was a white-faced clock with a single hand and this, when he turned on the current, began to revolve.

'At present it is impossible to be automatically exact,' he said, 'but soon I shall have perfected a meter which will instantly notify me that my leetle stone is cooked! You will understand that the whiteness and the brilliancy of the stone is a matter of temperature.'

Farther along the bench he showed them an experiment with a white sapphire, burying it on a small plate of sand which he heated electrically. At the end of the experiment, he lifted the stone with a pair of tweezers. The sapphire now sparkled with the rare brilliance of a diamond.

'But alas, it fades!' he said mournfully. 'Otherwise I should be a rich man, for nobody but experts can distinguish this from the real.'

Growing tired of sitting, they strolled around the 'factory', and Guelder pointed out various inventions of his that had directly led to the greater experiment.

'I suppose you realize that we shall get an offer from the big companies for this apparatus of yours,' said Sleser. 'They will want to do their own tinting. I reckon there are two millions in this scheme alone, apart from any speculation.'

Guelder said nothing. He was secretly amused, that nobody had made any suggestion as to the reward he should receive. Already they were speaking of the apparatus as proprietors.

This fact had already occurred to the business-like Sleser, and he drew his associates on one side at the first opportunity.

'We shall have to give this fellow a pretty substantial sum on account,' he said, 'and, of course, we must give him a big interest in the company.'

Guelder was drawn into the conference. He was very meek, almost humble, received their guarantee of £50,000 with every exhibition of gratitude. He was a heavy holder in the pool that had been formed and would have, they told him, an important interest in the Coloration Syndicate.

Nobody knew but he that he had already operated outside the pool, had broken faith with his partners even before the partnership was an accomplished fact. Julian was no man to be content with a few tens of thousands; his eyes were fixed on the million mark, and he would not be satisfied until he had reached that goal.

From time to time, they walked back to the buzzing instrument and watched curiously the little heap of white crystalline powder beneath which lay the genesis of an incomparable fortune. One of the watchers, standing by the window overlooking the river, remarked upon the ease with which a murder might be committed and the victim disposed of. Even the guest himself saw the grim possibility in his remark. He opened the window which looked out on the river. The rain was pelting down steadily. Far away showed the twinkling lights on the opposite shore.

'Shut the window, for God's sake!' said Sleser irritably.

'And don't talk about murder. This place gives me the creeps – what is that?'

In the darkness at the far end of the room two green orbs had appeared.

'My leetle cat,' chuckled Guelder, and whistled.

The white ghost form of the enormous animal came slowly into view; she rubbed herself against Guelder's leg, and then permitted him to stroke her ear.

'Gave me a start – phew!' Sleser wiped his streaming forehead with a large handkerchief and glanced fearfully around.

'Why the devil didn't you fix your laboratory somewhere up west, eh? There's something uncanny about this place. I wonder if anybody was ever murdered here?'

Even as he spoke he saw the big cat stand stiff, saw the fur rise and heard her low, angry purr, and then, like a streak of lightning, she leapt down the room and was instantly out of sight.

'It is nothing,' said Guelder, waving his hand airily. 'Her friend has trouble in the boat-house.' He pointed to the floor. 'Rats . . . there are many just now. Hundreds and hundreds of them, and when one leetle cat is in trouble she calls her brudder and sister – dat is all!'

Mr. Sleser wiped his neck under his collar, gazing uneasily at the dark end of the room.

'Uncanny,' he said thickly. 'Come on, let's get on with this. How long are you going to be?'

'Very soon now. Come back.'

He peered at the hand of the meter, gazed at a smaller instrument that looked like a voltmeter, and then at his watch.

'I don't know . . .' He was hesitant. 'Either it is now or never. If this experiment fails, gentlemen, again we must try. In science nothing comes instantly.'

He took a little porcelain bath, filled it very carefully with a white opaque fluid which he poured from a big bottle labelled 'Poison', and then, scraping off the dust that covered the diamond with a pair of tweezers, he lifted the stone and dropped it into the milky dish.

'In a minute now,' he said huskily.

That minute seemed like hours. There was no sound but their deep breathing. He had switched off the current, and the hum of the machine had died away, leaving a complete silence. He groped down into the fluid with his tweezers.

'Take that cloth, please . . .'

He pointed to a small yellow duster, and it was Sleser who obeyed his instructions.

'Now!'

He groped down with his tweezers, gripped the diamond, and deftly transferred it into the waiting cloth.

'Wipe it quickly . . .'

Sleser obeyed.

'Now look.'

The millionaire was staring at the thing in his palm. Dark yellow diamond there was no more: this was a thing of white and blue fire, beautiful to see.

'My God!' he muttered, and carried the stone under the light.

'Will it last?'

Guelder smiled.

'For efer!' he said emphatically.

The experiment was finished now. They brought the stone to the sitting-room where the lights were more brilliant. On Guelder's desk he had fitted a daylight lamp, and under this they crowded together to examine head to head this amazing gem.

'That's a white diamond – I'll stake my life on it!'

'May I keep this with me for twenty-four hours?'

Guelder shrugged.

'For twenty-four years, my frient!' he said humorously. 'As a yellow diamond it was worth maybe three hundred pounds.'

'It's worth four thousand as a white,' said Sleser huskily. 'I'll guarantee to sell it to a dealer for that. This is marvellous!'

There was a knock at the door. Guelder opened it.

'What is it?' he asked impatiently of the old woman.

'This stupid telephone has been ringing for hours,' said the phlegmatic Freda. 'I do not understand English, but they ask for Mr. Reef.'

Guelder caught Julian's eye and beckoned him.

'Phone,' said Guelder and then, in a low tone: 'What do

you think of me? Am I not beyond compare in science? Shall not all the peoples of the world talk of Rex Guelder, eh?'

'You're a marvellous fellow. Who is it wants me?'

'Ach!' said Guelder in disgust. 'Go mit Freda. She was your intellectuality!'

Julian was gone five minutes. He did not come back, but sent Freda for her master. They had a consultation in a low tone at the foot of the stairs and soon afterwards Julian left the house.

'Where's Reef gone?' asked one of the party when Guelder returned alone.

The Dutchman explained that Julian had been called away on a very urgent matter, but gave no further explanation. It was neither advisable nor expedient to say that at that moment Julian Reef was chasing a Rolls in Mr. Guelder's sports car, or what would be the likely outcome of that chase.

24

AFTER seeing Ursula home, Tony came back to his house more than a little perturbed. Elk had accompanied him to Hampstead and had asked to be dropped *en route*.

'It is rather a curious fact,' said Tony, 'and I haven't told you this before, that I have been followed for the past few days. Once I went back and tried to find the man; and if I'd caught him I'd have given him something that would rather have discouraged him!'

'In which case you'd have been pinched,' said Elk, calmly. 'Not even millionaires are allowed to beat up members of the C.I.D.'

'What's that?' said Tony, hardly believing his ears.

'It was one of my men who's been put on to look after you, Mr. Braid. I might as well tell you that I was afraid you might be committing suicide one of these days, and you're such a good feller that I didn't like to take the risk.'

'Do you seriously mean that I've been watched by a —?'

'Detective,' said Elk. 'And you've got to pretend not to notice him. He was behind us when we came out of Kirro's; he was the fellow that chased along the street and tried to get a car to follow the shooting gentleman. There's one thing I'd like to ask, Mr. Braid; is there anybody who knew you went to Woolwich tonight, or why you went to Woolwich?'

Tony shook his head.

'You told nobody – telephoned to nobody?'

'Except to Lady Ursula.'

'Tell your servants, by any chance?'

'Certainly not the maid, she sleeps out and I've only got one man – named Lein. He's not a very bright specimen and I certainly shouldn't have taken him into my confidence, the more so as I've given him a week's notice. He's a little too inquisitive.'

'Lein?' repeated Elk thoughtfully. 'How long has he been with you?'

'Only a month,' said Tony. 'He came with very good references.'

'Can anybody hear when you 'phone or when I 'phone?'

Tony smiled.

'If they stood outside the door and listened hard they could hear me, but I doubt if they could hear you. Good Lord! The extension!'

He told Elk of the bedroom instrument.

'Anybody who listened in there would of course hear the whole conversation. I never thought of that before. But it's very unlikely.'

'Nothing's very unlikely. I'll step inside and talk to Lein.'

'The man may be perfectly honest —' began Tony.

'No man is,' said Elk. 'I'm not; you're not, from what I hear. And I'll bet Lein has got twenty-eight convictions!'

When he confronted the rather nervous young man who came in answer to Tony's ring, Mr. Elk could not recognize a desperate criminal. If that had been possible he would have done so before, for he had an excellent memory. But, as he subsequently explained, the majority of criminals are not at all well known, and it is only the unfortunate few, comparatively, whom the police call by their family names.

'Where were you before, my son?' asked Elk.

The man hesitated just a fraction of a second too long.

'With Lord Ryslip.' He named a famous overseas Governor who, to Elk's knowledge, had been absent from England for five years.

He asked another question; the man floundered a little, then grew defiant and a little truculent.

'If you're saucy to me,' said Elk gently, 'I'll throw you through that window on to the iron spikes! You know me, my son?'

'Yes, sir, you're Sergeant Elk.'

Elk's eyes narrowed.

'Inspector, you poor out-of-date herring!'

And then the man made a mistake and blurted:

'They always call you sergeant.'

Elk looked at him steadily.

'An associate of thieves, eh? Who sent you here? Tell me why you listened in to Mr. Braid's conversation with me tonight, and then tell me who you 'phoned, or I'll put you in the cold, cold jug and you'll freeze to death!'

The man blustered and in the end abruptly left the room.

'Guilty,' said Elk, 'but I don't know what you can do with him. Now in the old days, when we had torture chambers in the Tower, which was the old-time Scotland Yard, we'd have got quite a lot of interesting things out of him, but they don't allow any third-degree in England.'

He came to his feet as he heard the street door bang. He was half-way to the door, but turned back.

'Getting impulsive in my old age,' he said, 'and I've got nothing to charge that bird with; I've an idea I can pick him up just when I want. Do you remember what I said over the phone? Did I mention the coat?'

Tony nodded.

'That was it. Did I mention the Honourable Mr. Julian Reef? I'll bet I did! And I'll bet that's who this feller telephoned – probably at Greenwich. That's an old trick of Reef's – oh yes, he's done it before.'

There and then he told Tony quite a lot about Mr. Julian

Reef that he had never heard before. They were not nice stories; one at least was very ugly.

'It's a funny business, this detectivizing,' said Elk. 'We know so much more about people than they think we know, or they'd like us to know. There are men in the West End tonight who'd go white-haired if they knew just what Scotland Yard was thinking of them. They'll never be pinched perhaps, but then they don't do things for which people are pinched. Half the sin in the world is legal, and it's the worst half, as I can prove.'

He left Anthony Braid to pass a sleepless and troubled night. At four o'clock in the morning he rose and walked to his bedroom window. It was still raining and below, in the dim light of dawn, he saw a sturdy figure standing in the shadow of a doorway, smoking a pipe. Tony guessed that it was his watcher, and waved a cheery salute, to which the unknown man responded. He made himself a cup of coffee. For some reason which he could not understand, his mind was occupied by Ursula Frensham.

He felt uncomfortable about her, for no especial reason, unless that attempted murder of the previous night had made more acute his sense of danger.

He finished the coffee and dressed; five minutes later he was in the street. The detective on duty walked across the road to greet him.

'You're rather early this morning, Mr. Braid.'

'I'm taking a run to Hampstead. Would you like to come?'

'I've got to come,' said the other good-naturedly. 'I'm glad Mr. Elk told you. If you don't mind my saying so, you've been rather a nuisance, Mr. Braid; you're such a difficult man to trail.'

He accompanied Tony to the garage in the mews, and together they brought out the convertible.

'Is there any reason for your going to Hampstead?' asked the detective when they were on their way.

'None at all,' said Tony guiltily.

He felt exceedingly foolish; certainly had not the courage to tell the man by his side on what a futile errand they were bound.

They turned into Regent's Park, the gates of which had just

been opened, and came along the broad Outer Circle. As they went over the bridge which spans the canal at the foot of Avenue Road, Tony saw a man leaning over the iron rail, looking intently into the water and he could have sworn he recognized the figure. It was rendered more shapeless by a heavy waterproof, the collar of which was turned up to the ears. Its owner evinced no curiosity as to the occupant of the car that was abroad so early in the morning. Moreover, and this looked suspicious to Tony, he deliberately turned his head away so that his face could not be seen.

On the other side of the bridge was a long-bodied sports car, drawn up so far along the road that unless he had stopped his own vehicle and got out to examine it, it was impossible to see the number.

'That looked like Mr. Guelder,' said the detective.

'I thought it did. Do you know him?'

'I've seen him. That was his car along the road, wasn't it? Did you see it last night, sir?'

Tony shook his head.

'Neither did I, but from the height at which the man fired I could swear it was a sports model, the same as that one. But, of course, it couldn't have been Mr. Guelder: he was at his house when it happened.'

'How do you know?' asked Tony in surprise.

The detective smiled.

'At the Yard we swear by Inspector Elk's method – which is to inquire,' he said drily. 'And we inquired long before you went to sleep, Mr. Braid.'

They ran up the Avenue on to the Heath and turned into the road where Ursula's house occupied a corner site. Tony got out and walked round the two sides of the house. He knew which was Ursula's window; it was open at the top. To his surprise he saw a light burning and when he continued his walk and came into view of the front door, he saw that there was a light also in the hall. It was a quarter past five; the maid would not be up for another two hours.

He was hesitating what to do when he heard her cool voice hail him and saw her walking towards him, fully dressed.

'So that was why you didn't answer my telephone call!' she said.

'What on earth are you doing up at this hour?' he asked.
She laughed.
'I was called up at two o'clock to receive a proposal of marriage,' she said, 'and naturally I haven't been to sleep since. I am rather glad I haven't, for the gentleman who proposed over the phone has been patrolling up and down outside the house since daybreak.'

Tony stared at her incredulously.

'Not – surely not Guelder? No, that would be monstrous.'

She nodded.

'Mr. Guelder it was,' she said, and then her voice broke and her self-control deserted her.

In another instant she was in Tony's arms, sobbing:

'Oh, Tony, it was horrible – horrible!'

25

It was some little time before she was calm enough to tell what had happened. She had heard the phone ringing and had thought that it might have something to do with her visit to Woolwich, and then she heard Guelder's voice.

'He was very apologetic and nice, and I couldn't very well hang up until I knew what had happened. I thought it might be something about Julian. And then, Tony, he began making the wildest statements. He said he was worth a million – or two, I'm not sure which – that he would be the richest man in England before a year was over, and he was going to build a palace where the woman of his heart would reign as a queen. I didn't understand all he said. Sometimes he lapsed into Dutch and I couldn't make head or tail of what he was saying. And then, before I knew what was happening, he was asking me to marry him. I just stood there petrified, not able to speak. He said he'd loved me ever since he'd seen me – it was ghastly . . . the things he said . . . At last I came back to my senses and cut him off, but of course it was impossible to go to sleep again. Day was breaking when I looked out of my window and then, to my horror, I saw him slowly strolling up and down the road. He saw me, too, and kissed his hand – he must have been drunk.'

Tony remembered the man on the bridge.

'Then it *was* Guelder!' he said.

'You haven't seen him?' she asked quickly.

Tony told her of the man who was standing on the bridge.

'I think I'll go back and have a talk with Mr. Guelder,' he said, but she caught his arm.

'You'll do nothing of the kind. You mustn't, Tony! I want you to keep away from him, not to quarrel with him. There's something diabolical about that man. It was his awful influence I could feel last night in Greenwich. It wasn't the street, it was the spirit of this terrible man. If he ever touched me again I think I should die.'

'If he ever touches you again,' said Tony grimly, 'I think *he* will die!'

The maid brought them coffee and biscuits, and as they sat in the little library Tony tried to get her to tell him all that Guelder had said, but resolutely she refused to discuss the matter.

'All I remember is that he was a millionaire, and that it's something about diamonds, and he said he was the greatest inventor of the age. And, Tony, you're not to see him – do you hear?'

He shook his head.

'I'm afraid I've got to see him, Ursula. There mustn't be a repetition of that experience.'

'I think he must be mad – I'm sure that it was he who fired at you last night.'

Tony, who was equally sure that Guelder was innocent in that matter, said nothing. For to exculpate the Dutchman involved many explanations.

Was Guelder really mad? he wondered, on his way back to his house. There was nothing very extraordinary about his falling in love with Ursula. It was rather horrible, but it was normal, and this man was something of a squire of dames. If rumour spoke truly, he had never flown quite so high as Ursula Frensham. He had found his affinities in a lower sphere; he was a man of low tastes and more than a little revolting. But Guelder must be interviewed, and fervently Tony prayed that in that interview he would be able to keep his hands in his pockets.

Julian . . . did he know of his partner's predilection? Tony had to consider this possibility. Somehow, though he had a very poor opinion of Julian Reef, he could not credit him with the knowledge of Guelder's infatuation. Julian himself had had very definite ideas about Ursula's matrimonial future and it was unlikely, indeed impossible, that he would for a moment countenance the thing that had happened last night.

He got home, had a bath and shaved, and was breakfasting when Mr. Sleser was announced. The millionaire was no close friend of Tony's; they had had business dealings and on one occasion, which Tony had forgotten, he had been of some service to this thickset and self-made man for whom he had a very high respect.

'Have you breakfasted?' asked Tony.

The thickset gentleman nodded as he pulled up a chair to the table.

'I'm the last man in the world you expected to see, Braid,' he smiled amiably. 'What I've been debating with myself since six o'clock is whether I should let you in or leave you out. You obliged me once, and I never forget a pal. You're a friend of Reef's?'

'Emphatically I am not!' said Tony. 'I'm glad you asked me, because at the back of my mind I have an idea you're associated with him in a certain operation.'

Sleser nodded.

'He's not everybody's money,' he said, 'but in a way he's useful. He may be very, very useful – I don't know yet. Do you know his partner – or whatever he is?'

'Guelder?'

'The Dutchman – yes. Clever devil, isn't he?'

'I believe he is,' said Tony, 'as a scientist. There's a rumour in the City that he has discovered a method of making diamonds.'

Sleser chuckled at this.

'Not quite! I'd hate to see that happen, though I loathe your crowd.'

He was silent for a long time, evidently turning the matter over in his mind, and at last he said:

'I'm not a whale on history, but wasn't there a fellow who went along and sold Guy Fawkes by telling his friends to keep away from Parliament?'

'There was such a man,' smiled Tony.

'I am he,' said Sleser with emphasis. 'You did me a good turn – I want to do you one. Keep out of the diamond market! If you've any holdings, sell! The slump yesterday was only child's play to what will come today. I'm telling you this over your own table; though I can't very well ask you to keep it to yourself, I know you enough to believe that you will. They call you The Twister in the City' – his eyes twinkled – 'well, I've never seen you put a twist on any man yet and I don't expect you to start with me.'

Tony looked at him thoughtfully.

'I'd like to know a little more about this slump. What is behind it, Sleser? Perhaps I may be able to do you another good turn.'

'Very likely,' said Sleser, and putting his hand in his pocket, he took out a fat pocket-book. 'I'm showing you something that no outsider has seen.'

He took from the pocket-book a blue paper and opened it carefully. Inside was a little pad of cottonwool, and this he unrolled.

'What do you think of that?'

Tony took the diamond and held it against the sleeve of his coat.

'She's rather a beauty! Have you found a new mine?' he asked with a faint smile.

Sleser shook his head.

'What is that worth? You know something about these things.'

Tony considered.

'Roughly four thousand pounds,' he said, and the stout man nodded.

'You're within five pounds of it. Now tell me: what would that stone be worth if it were yellow or had a bad tint?'

On this subject Tony was something of an authority.

'It would be worth about three hundred pounds, and – good God!' He stared at his visitor. 'Yellow diamonds! Guelder has been buying them for months, and I have been wondering what his game was. That's not a recoloured diamond . . . is that the discovery?'

Again Sleser nodded.

'Last night,' he said impressively, 'that was yellow. I saw it turn white under my own eyes. There's no doubt about it, this man has made a discovery which will revolutionize the diamond market, will send present values down fifty per cent. Don't you realize, Braid, what this means? Only one diamond in seven is a perfect white stone; this brings even the duds up to top value, it increases the output by six or sevenfold.'

Tony was turning the stone over and over in his hand. Presently he put it down, went to his bureau, and brought out a magnifying glass; the amused Mr. Sleser watched him.

'I've tried all that stuff. I've had it under a microscope. I got the cleverest people in London out of bed at two this morning and made a thorough examination. It's white through and through; you can't fault it. Anyway, it's been done before, you know – scientists have turned white diamonds pink; why shouldn't they turn yellow ones white? Well, what are you going to do? If you're wise, you'll sell every share you hold. The only thing I ask is that you'll keep the secret about the colour changing till twelve o'clock. By then I shall have a statement ready for the Press.'

He put the diamond back in its cottonwool swathing and restored it to his pocket-book.

'That's about all, I think,' he said, as he rose and offered his hand. 'You and I are quits over that African Transport stock you got me out of. If you're not sensible, I'll make money out of you. If you're wise, you'll make money out of me. I'm going to give the Kimberley crowd the biggest kick in the pants they've ever had . . . so long!'

With a nod he left.

Tony sat before the remains of his breakfast, and thought more quickly and more logically than he had ever done in his life. His own fortune was largely wrapped up in the diamond industry and there could be no question at all that this invention of Guelder's represented the greatest danger that had ever threatened diamond finance.

He had half promised his friends not to sell, and a half promise, with Tony Braid, was any other man's deed bond. He knew exactly what would be the effect of this news upon the market, unprepared as the diamond financiers were for the disclosure. Shares would drop to a record low level. He had only to ring up his broker and order him to sell, not only the stocks he held but the stocks he would sell for delivery, to make himself half a million before nightfall. He thought the matter over: in his mind's eye all the time he saw that square diamond winking and leering at him from the table.

His coffee was cold: he rang for a new pot, and before it was served he put through a call to the chief of the diamond men.

'I think you must be prepared for a big slump this morning,' he said. 'I can tell you no more.'

'You can't give me a reason?' asked the man at the other end.

'No, I can't. I'm practically pledged to silence. Personally, I'm not a seller, I'm a buyer. I suppose it's an act of lunacy on my part, but I'm going in to support the market, and I want your help – I may want half a million – I have undeveloped platinum fields in the north of Transvaal which will be worth that amount. Will you stake me half a million?'

'To support the market – yes. Tell your banker to get in touch with mine . . . I know your platinums, so you needn't send me any description. If you come through without being hurt, I'd like a twenty-five per cent interest in that property.'

Tony named a price and in two minutes the deal was through. And now, irrespective of stocks and shares, or the tragic fall of diamonds, he had a personal matter which required his immediate attention.

Before business began on 'Change he passed into the block which housed Julian Reef and his multifarious schemes. He saw at a glance when he came to the outer office that the clerical staff had been augmented. There was an atmosphere of unusual activity and something of the electrical influence of this gigantic battle which was being waged in Throgmorton Street had affected the most junior of clerks.

26

'MR. REEF is in, sir, but I don't know whether he can see you without an appointment.'

There was a certain pomposity and importance in that announcement which made Tony smile.

'Take my card,' he said, well knowing that the clerk had recognized him and was passing on to him a little of his employer's insolence.

Julian kept him waiting for ten minutes, an unfortunate circumstance, as it proved, for half that time had elapsed when there came into the railed space where visitors waited a thin little man, with an old-fashioned hat and very large, broad-toed shoes.

'I must see Mr.—' – he consulted a card – 'Mr. Rex Guelder. It is very important. Will you tell him Mr. Samer from Troubridge wishes to see him at once? And will you please tell him it is most urgent? I've come up from Troubridge this morning especially to see him.'

'I don't know whether Mr. Guelder is here,' said the clerk. 'Take a seat.'

The old man sat down breathlessly and mopped his bald forehead. He was talkative, in the way of a shy man amongst strangers.

'I left at five o'clock this morning,' he said. 'I was very fortunate to get a train. I haven't been to London for thirty-seven years ... the place has changed.'

'Terribly,' admitted Tony. 'You live at Troubridge?'

'Yes, sir,' said the old man with some satisfaction. 'We have been established in Troubridge for two hundred and thirty-five years. I doubt if there's any other firm in the town with our record. The business has passed from father to son, and will go eventually to my boy, who is fifty-two and subsequently, I hope, to my grandson, who is also in the business.'

Tony was about to ask the gentleman from Troubridge what his particular business was, but at that moment he was summoned to the august presence of Julian.

Julian was a man transfigured. He moved in an atmosphere of

confidence that was almost, Tony told himself, cockiness. And his very reception of his visitor revealed his changed outlook. Yet behind his lordliness, Tony – wise in the ways of men – detected a subtle uneasiness; it almost seemed as though he had to force himself to meet the eyes of the caller.

'Sorry to keep you waiting, Braid, but I'm terribly busy just now and I hope your business won't take you very long. The truth is that for the last week I've been working day and night.'

'You ought to find time to go to a shooting-gallery,' said Tony. 'Your marksmanship leaves something to be desired.'

Julian forced a laugh.

'I saw in the papers that there'd been what they call a shooting affray, that somebody had loosed off a couple of rounds at "a famous detective". I presume that was Elk?'

'The newspaper didn't say a couple of rounds; it said one round,' said Tony coolly, 'and only one newspaper had the report – probably you're better informed.'

Julian checked a protest: he had already said too much.

'What do you want now?'

'I wish to see your Mr. Guelder; I have a bone to pick with him.'

Julian looked bored.

'My dear fellow,' he said wearily, 'why bother me with your private feuds? Anyway, Guelder isn't here. He's gone into the country for a day and I don't expect to see him until tomorrow. If that's all you want—' He rose significantly, and looked at the door.

'That is not quite all,' said Tony. 'I suppose you know that your Dutch friend is making himself objectionable to Ursula Frensham.'

Evidently he didn't know, for his expression changed.

'What do you mean?'

'I mean that he called her up in the night and proposed marriage to her over the telephone. I don't know whether he was drunk, or suffering from the exuberance of his new discovery.'

He saw Julian start.

'I know all about it. Sleser came to me this morning, but I'm not using my information till it is published in the newspapers.'

'He called up Ursula—'

'He called up Lady Ursula on the telephone and proposed marriage to her. Are you aware of his – tender feelings?'

Julian dropped his eyes.

'No,' he said doggedly. 'Anyway, I can't be expected to control Guelder out of business hours.'

Yet Tony was judge enough of humanity to know that the news had shocked him.

'What does Ursula say about it?' he asked, not raising his eyes.

'Naturally she is not flattered. I came today to see Guelder and tell him that if that is repeated I'll flog him until he's sorry. And that also applies, Julian Reef, to vicarious gunmen who take pot-shots at me in the early hours of the morning.'

Julian was about to speak, but Tony went on:

'You will also be interested to learn that your friend the valet has been fired. But you probably know that. I expect he came bleating to you this morning. If you're anxious to find out what is happening in my house, I'll arrange to have a special bulletin prepared and delivered to you twice daily!'

'I don't know what you're talking about,' said Julian sulkily. 'I think you're mad half the time. Really, you're a most extraordinary fellow! Anyway, Guelder's not here. You'd better come and have your quarrel with him when he is. I suppose you're selling diamonds? You wouldn't be you if you didn't. Sleser was a fool to tell you.'

'I'll pass on the information,' said Tony, and Julian's look of alarm showed him exactly the awe in which he stood of the great gambler.

As he came out the clerk entered and he heard Julian say:

'Tell him to come tomorrow – I don't want to see anybody now or later.'

The message was delivered to the old man in the railed space across the room.

'Oh, dear; oh, dear!' he said, gathering up his umbrella and his brown bag. 'I don't know what I shall do – her ladyship will never forgive me.'

The curiosity of Tony was piqued. He held the door open for the gentleman from Troubridge and followed him down into the street.

'It's a most distressing thing.' He had to tell his trouble to somebody, it seemed. 'I've never had such a thing happen to me in all the years I've been in business. If I could only see Mr. Guelder for a few minutes—'

'I should like to see Mr. Guelder for a few minutes too,' said Tony grimly. And then, touched by the old man's distress, 'Could I help you in any way?'

Mr. Samer shook his head.

'I'm afraid you can't. You see, when I sold the diamond to Mr. Guelder I did so in good faith. I hadn't realized the terrible mistake my assistant had made.'

Tony was all attention now.

'Come along over to my club,' he said. 'Perhaps I *can* help you.'

Uttering disjointed words of thanks, Mr. Samer trotted by his side and in the smoke-room of a City club, deserted at this time of the morning, he told his story.

There was a great lady who lived near Troubridge, no less than the Duchess of Handfield. He, Mr. Samer, kept a big jeweller's shop and carried a large stock. He and his forefathers had done repairs for Her Grace's family for hundreds of years. When she sent her diamond ring to be reset, he had taken out the stone very carefully and locked it in his safe. There were other stones which were for sale, and in his temporary absence his assistant (he did not say his son, but Tony gathered that that was mere family pride) had been interviewed by a gentleman from London, who was anxious to buy a square, cushion-shaped diamond.

'What's that?' said Tony quickly. 'Can you tell me the weight?'

'Ten carats,' said the jeweller, 'a trifle over. I have the exact weight on the back of the photograph.'

'Go on,' said Tony.

The assistant was naturally flattered when Mr. Guelder said he had heard of the stocks that were carried by the jeweller, and he was anxious to buy a big stone for an engagement ring. The assistant unlocked the safe, took out a number of stones and, most unfortunately, found the Duchess's diamond; thinking it was available he had offered it for sale. On the paper in which it was wrapped had been written, in Mr. Samer's own handwriting, '£4,000' – that being the amount of the short-time insurance he had taken out to guarantee himself against burglary. For £4,000 the stone had changed hands. Mr. Guelder had paid in banknotes, and had taken his purchase to London. And now the Duchess, who had been abroad, had written to say she was coming home and she hoped the ring would be ready for her.

'And, Mr—, I didn't catch your name – Mr. Braid, is it? – not the racing Mr. Braid? Dear me! I sometimes have a little flutter myself, not to any very great extent, not sufficient to keep myself interested in what I would call the sport of kings. Well, Mr. Braid, that is the position. I must induce Mr. Guelder to let me have the stone back – I don't mind paying him a hundred pounds on top of the price he paid.'

'Can you describe the diamond a little more carefully?'

'I can show you a photograph of it,' said Mr. Samer eagerly.

He had it, of all places, in his waistcoat pocket; it was, he said, his practice – and had been the practice of his father – to photograph all important stones that passed through their hands. His great-grandfather had employed an artist to sketch them for he had lived in the days when photography was in its infancy.

Tony looked at the photograph, a slip of print pasted on a thick strip of cardboard, and his heart leapt.

'I think I can get you back your stone,' he said, and Mr. Samer almost fell upon his neck with gratitude.

As they went out Tony paused in the hall to look at the tape messages that were coming through.

'Looking for diamonds, Mr. Braid?' said the porter and pointed to a strip on a green board.

Diamonds were falling sensationally. Stocks that had stood at £12 on the previous day were now at 9 and 8¾.

'Excuse me a moment while I telephone,' he said to his new friend.

Going into one of the booths he called his broker, and gave him explicit instructions. He named three stocks.

'Buy,' he said, 'and don't stop buying until my account is set back a million. No, you can go to a million and a half.'

'But the market is falling, Mr. Braid,' said the agonized broker 'Don't you think it would be better—'

'Buy till you're tired,' said Tony.

He came out and collected the distraught jeweller and hailed a taxi. They drove to the end of Lombard Street, where the Sleser Consolidated Building lifted its grey head high above its fellows, and taking the elevator to the top floor, Tony had the good fortune to buttonhole Sleser's private secretary, a man with whom he was acquainted.

'I'm very sorry, Mr. Braid, but I don't think Mr. Sleser will see you. He's in up to his eyes in the diamond business.'

'People who go in up to their eyes,' said Tony, 'invariably get drowned. Will you tell him I'm here and that I've come in the capacity of life-saver?'

The secretary smiled.

'Are you a seller?' he asked confidentially. 'You should be, Mr. Braid! Mr. Sleser told me to get on to you half an hour ago, but I couldn't find you at home. I'll ask if he will see you.'

'And my friend Mr. Samer,' said Tony.

The secretary looked a little dubious at this, but went away and carried the message. A few minutes later he came back and beckoned Tony through his office to the private room of the great speculator.

27

MR. SLESER sat at his huge desk, an incongruous pipe in his mouth; and the room reeked with the pungent odour of burnt shag.

'Come in, Braid.'

'This is Mr. Samer,' said Tony.

'Glad to meet you. I can give you exactly two minutes.'

'It won't be enough,' said Tony, his eyes gleaming. 'If you think that it is, just fire us out. Have you got that diamond with you?'

Sleser frowned.

'Yes,' he said slowly. 'What do you want?'

'Our friend here is a jeweller.'

Sleser lay back in his chair and laughed.

'What a sceptical old devil you are! Couldn't believe your own eyes, eh? Well, I don't think I can even give you two minutes, but I'll show you the stone.'

He unlocked the safe, took out a small brown case and opened it. The oblong diamond glittered from its blue velvet bed.

'That's it!' cried Mr. Samer tremulously. 'Thank heaven I've found it . . . this has saved my reputation, Mr. Braid!'

Sleser was gaping at him.

'What's this?' he asked, and frowned at Tony Braid.

'I can tell you in a few minutes. That diamond was purchased from this gentleman by Rex Guelder two or three days ago,' said Tony, quietly. 'It was sold by mistake. It really belongs to the Duchess of Handfield, she had sent the stone to be reset and it was sold by mistake—'

'By an assistant,' murmured Mr. Samer.

Sleser pushed back his chair from the desk.

'Let me get this right. You recognize this stone as one you sold to Mr. Guelder two or three days ago?'

'My assistant,' corrected Mr. Samer. 'The gentleman came and said he wanted a diamond of a special shape: he was searching England for it, because he wanted to match it with a yellow diamond that he had of similar shape and weight. Not exactly the same weight, as far as I can gather, but—'

'Do you know the weight of this?'

Mr. Samer produced his little photograph again, on the back of which were written figures that only he could understand.

Sleser went to the window, where, under a glass case, stood a delicate balance. He laid the diamond on one side and placed some tiny flat weights in the other.

'Exactly,' he said, and drew a long breath.

For a time that seemed an eternity, no sound was heard; and

then Mr. Sleser pressed a bell. His secretary appeared, with the intention of showing out his visitors.

'Shut the door,' said Sleser. 'Phone the bank and stop payment of that cheque for fifty thousand I drew for Guelder. Phone every broker you know to stop selling and to buy exactly the same stocks. Tell them to buy and not to stop. Thank you; that is all.'

He took up the pipe he had put on the desk, lit it and puffed out a cloud of rank smoke.

'Your idea of the aristocracy will go down a peg, Mr. Samer, but I am a personal friend of the Duchess of Handfield, and I'll see that no trouble comes to you through this stone. I want it for a day or two, after which it will be returned to you. Her Grace is in Paris; as a matter of fact, I heard from her this morning. I'll get her on the phone and find out how long she's staying. If she's coming over immediately, I'll tell her the truth. If she isn't – well, you can have your stone back. Thank you.'

He put out his hand and gripped the little man with such vehemence that Mr. Samer stood on one leg.

'You can find your way out, sir? I want you, Mr. Braid.'

When the little jeweller had gone:

'That's another one I owe you, Braid. I have a serious liking for "twisters". That swine double-crossed us last night – think of it: a lot of grown men caught by a thimblerigger. It wouldn't have deceived a schoolboy at a Maskelyne and Devant show. What he did, of course, was to change one stone for another, and he fixed a blue spark to frighten us, to hide the fact that the substitution was being made. It's clear to me – but I'm about ten hours late. You and I will have a little talk with Mr. Guelder.'

'He's not in his office —' began Tony.

'Stuff!' said the other. 'He's phoned me twice this morning!'

No clerk of Julian's dared arrest the progress of the great Sleser as he strode across the outer office and, pushing open the door of Reef's private room, walked in, followed by Tony.

Julian was not alone. Mr. Guelder sat at ease in a deep armchair, a cigar between his teeth. He beamed at the sight of Sleser, but the smile faded when Tony Braid came into view.

'Shut the door, Braid, will you?'

Sleser took out a case from his pocket, opened it, and exposed the diamond.

'You made this last night, didn't you, Guelder?'

'Yes, zat was the stone,' said Guelder, complacently.

Sleser looked at Julian.

'Were you in this swindle?'

'Swindle?' gasped Julian Reef, turning pale. 'What do you mean? There was no swindle – you saw it with your own eyes. If you believe this fellow' – his accusing finger shot out towards Tony – 'naturally you'll believe it was a swindle. But you saw it —'

'I'm not believing him, I'm believing my eyes and my ears,' said the other curtly. 'This stone was bought from a man called Samer, of Troubridge. I can quite understand that for his spectacular experiment your Dutch pal wanted a stone of a unique shape. He had the yellow one all right, and was trying to match it up in the country. He bought this diamond for four thousand pounds.'

'Zat is a damned lie!' screamed Guelder. 'I make it mit my science – you saw me – you cannot believe what you see —'

'You rang the changes, you dirty crook,' roared Sleser. 'I shall be the laughing-stock of the City, and if it weren't for making myself the laughing-stock of the world, I'd jail you both!'

'I'm not in this.' Julian Reef's pallor, his vehemence, his almost despair, supported his protest. 'If that is true ... my God, it can't be true! You didn't do that, Guelder?'

Mr. Guelder was calmer now.

'If your mind is greater than dis matter – well' – he shrugged his shoulders – 'I am scientist, not psychologist. You see mit your own eyes, you do not believe, you listen to this twisting person —'

He stepped back suddenly behind the desk.

'I'm not going to hit you,' said Tony, 'but if you ever bother Lady Ursula Frensham again, I shall probably wring your neck.'

But Julian was not thinking of Ursula: he was thinking of his tremendous commitments, of the extravagant orders he had given, which had been reluctantly accepted by brokers, to sell diamond shares; he was thinking of his few friends who had staked their money on this trickster. He glared for a second at the Dutchman, and then with a scream of rage he leapt at him. It was Sleser who pulled them apart and flung the red-haired man back to the wall.

'Do your murder when I'm not here!' he growled. 'Come along, Braid; let's see what's happening on 'Change – if I get out of this at the cost of a million, I'll be a lucky man.'

As they were going down the stairs, he asked:

'I suppose you've told your pals about the fake?'

'No,' said Tony. He was a little ashamed that he had forgotten the men whom he regarded as his own party. 'I don't think that matters, though – they weren't selling.'

'Then there's a hope for me,' said Sleser.

It was a very slender hope, he saw when they got to the club. Diamond shares were soaring with as great rapidity as they had fallen.

He took the diamond out of his pocket, kissed it extravagantly, and handed it to Tony.

'Good-bye a million!' he said. 'I'm taking farewell of you. Keep that stone – I'll square the duchess.'

'You're very confident,' smiled Tony.

'I ought to be,' said the big man morosely. 'I gave it to her originally – like a fool I never recognized it!'

'You're wanted on the phone, Mr. Sleser.'

The millionaire went away, and came back in a few seconds with an unpleasant grin on his face.

'That was from the office,' he said. 'I gave Guelder an open cheque – he cashed it as soon as the bank opened. When he's hanged I wonder if the Sheriff will let me go to the execution. I haven't had a good laugh for years.'

28

THE rain had cleared off, and Ursula went for a walk on the Heath. She did not see the earlier editions of the evening newspapers, knew nothing of the war that had been waged in the City, of the staggering losses and tremendous gains registered on both sides; did not even associate Tony with the battle when rumour of the fray came to her.

It was only in the nature of things that he should win, for his lucky star was in the ascendant. By nightfall he would not dare compute his gains during that day of strife, when half a dozen firms, three of them of long-standing, went smash; and when the heads of the great banks regarded the situation so seriously that they met to formulate a plan to meet further trouble on the morrow.

It was nearly lunch-time when Ursula came back, to find Elk sitting on the step before the lawn window, smoking a cigar the shape of which she thought she recognized, and reading an evening edition.

He walked slowly to meet her.

'I asked that maid of yours to find me a smoke, Lady Ursula,' he said apologetically. 'I knew you wouldn't like me to be sitting here cold, and I told her to bring the cheapest you'd got in the house. Ask her yourself if you doubt my word. I said "Mary, or whatever your name is, don't bring me any of those expensive ones, bring me something worth about five cents".' (Elk had once been to America on a trip to bring back a fugitive swindler, and had acquired the currency of the country.)

'She brought you the cheapest and the best. I don't know whether I'm very glad to see you, Mr. Elk. Is there any trouble?'

Elk shook his head.

'Never have any trouble nowadays. Everybody's getting so law-abiding that we're thinking of reducing the police force.'

She asked him to stay to lunch, but he declined the invitation.

'There's just a few questions I wanted to put to you, Lady

Ursula,' he said, following her into the library. 'Mainly on things you know nothing about. But you might. You had fifty thousand pounds left you some time ago —'

'It has gone now, Mr. Elk,' she said, with a rueful smile.

'I know,' said Elk. 'There was a sort of fund formed, wasn't there? Mr. Reef had the handling of it and it sort of disappeared. Your father was very keen on that fund of yours, wasn't he?'

'I think so – I'm sure he was. Mr. Reef handed him the shares some time before his death.'

Elk's face was a mask.

'So I'm told. But suppose your father found there wasn't any shares; suppose, for the sake of argument, and libelling nobody, he found all this beautiful stock that had been bought for you had been sold and just punk stuff put in its place? He'd be a bit annoyed, wouldn't he?'

She hesitated.

'Don't mind telling me, regard me as your Uncle Joe,' suggested Elk. 'I only want to get the psychology of it. We're strong for psychology at the Yard just now.'

'Yes, he would be more than angry,' she said. 'My father was a very stern man. He would be furious. He would never have forgiven Julian. He would have —'

She hesitated again.

'Had him pinched?' suggested Elk.

'Arrested? I really think he would,' she said frankly. 'It may be true that he wanted the shares to cover his own overdraft, but I'm sure he would never dream of robbing me of a penny: he would have died first.'

'Exactly,' nodded Elk. 'If he found those shares were punk – which is French for *na poo* – and he wanted them for himself, and he thought this man Reef was robbing you . . ."

He waited expectantly.

'There's another thing I wanted to know, is there any place in this house where his lordship kept private papers?'

'There's a safe in the study,' she said, 'behind one of the panels. I only discovered it the other day. But he kept nothing valuable there – I opened it and it was empty. It was easy to find the key: Father kept it on a chain-ring.'

'Nothing there at all?' Elk shook his head, anticipating the answer, 'Nothing!'

'That is, nothing except —'

She pulled open a drawer.

'I put them here.' She took out three or four papers, 'One of them is a list of the shares you were talking about just now – my shares. But I think Mr. Braid has that.'

Elk examined the three documents. The first had no importance, nor the third. The second contained, as Ursula said, a list of the shares, and something more. Beneath were the words 'Received the above' and Julian Reef's signature.

'That's what I wanted,' said Elk, with satisfaction. 'That is what I call Exhibit Q. If you don't mind, I'll take it away with me, Lady Ursula.'

'Have you seen Mr. Reef this morning – about his coat?'

Elk shook his head.

'No. I expect Mr. Reef's so occupied with buying and selling diamonds that he hasn't any time to bother his head about old clothes. You haven't mentioned it to him, I suppose?'

'You asked me not to,' she smiled; 'and of course, I haven't seen him.'

'I thought you might have forgot,' said Elk. 'Do you know where I can find Mr. Braid? – I see you don't. Why I asked you the Lord knows! Anyone would think, to hear me talk to you, you were his young lady! Regular air-raid's going on in the City. Shares are popping up and shares are crashing down – heavy casualties on all sides.'

'On the Stock Exchange?' she asked, her mind going to Julian.

'Diamond shares,' said Elk. 'That's where the battle rages. On the rest of the front there's nothing to report. I often wish I'd been born a stockbroker. Figures are my speciality, and I could easily learn how to drive a car to Brighton.'

He lingered a while as if he had something further to say, and after a while it came.

'It's no use asking you about that coat of Mr. Reef's, I suppose? How often have you seen him wearing it?'

'Only once,' she said. 'I think it was a new one.'

'I know how new it is,' said Elk. 'The question is . . .' he was going to say something, but changed his mind. 'I'll be getting along now, Lady Ursula. Thank you for your invitation to dinner, but I never eat at midday; it makes me sleepy. And thank you for the cigars.'

Previously he had only mentioned one cigar, but she had already seen the reserve sticking out of his handkerchief pocket.

He arrived at Tony Braid's house simultaneously with the owner.

'Got no staff, have you?' said Elk. 'Have you been behind the lines this morning, Mr. Braid?'

'I've been battling with the rest of them,' said Tony, good-humouredly; 'but I was, so to speak, in a tank.'

'Made a couple of millions, I suppose?' said Elk, with a cluck of wonder. 'Poor soul! I wouldn't have the weight of your income-tax on my mind!'

'Do you want to see me?' asked Tony.

Elk scratched his chin.

'I've just refused an invitation to dinner with a lady, and if you go and tell her that I've wished myself on you she'll never forgive me.'

Tony knew from the detective's manner that he had something important to tell him. It was only by chance that he had come back to lunch: usually he went to his club, as he told Elk.

'If you hadn't been here I'd have called at the club. So you couldn't have missed standing me a dinner – lunch, I mean. I never can get used to society meals. In the course of the engagement this morning did you come across the mangled corpse of Mr. Julian Reef?'

'I saw him for a few moments, yes.' It was rather an ugly memory he had carried away of the debonair Julian, and he was not very anxious to discuss that scene at the office.

Elk asked no further questions till he was through lunch. A maid had taken away his last plate . . .

'Is she coming back again?'

'Why? No, if you don't want her to. She'll bring the coffee, but that can be delayed.'

'I'd rather have you all to myself for a little while,' said Elk, gently.

Tony rang the bell and gave the necessary instructions.

'It's about this fellow Reef,' said Elk. 'I will probably be taking him tonight.'

Tony said nothing. He had half expected the news. They sat without speaking for a little time, and then Tony said:

'I suppose it's unnecessary for me to ask on what charge?'

Elk stared at him thoughtfully.

'I think it *is* unnecessary, Mr. Braid.' he said quietly. 'I think you know almost as much about the case as I know; but in case you don't, I'm telling you that I shall charge Julian Reef with the wilful murder of Lord Frensham by shooting him with a revolver.'

In the tense silence which followed, Tony could hear the ticking of the clock on the mantelpiece.

'I presume you have plenty of evidence to substantiate your charge?' he said.

Elk nodded.

'Plenty. I had enough suspicion at the inquest. But suspicion isn't evidence.'

'What do you think happened?' asked Tony.

He was wondering how Ursula would receive this news and his heart ached for the girl. The wound might have been slight or deep, but it had closed; and now the Frensham case was to be redecorated with the most ugly colouring.

'In the first place,' said Elk, 'this man Reef was pretty desperate. Frensham had asked him for certain shares, which Reef had sold and applied to his own use. I don't think there's any doubt that Frensham wanted them to lodge against an overdraft; but probably he saw daylight, because he was not the kind of man who would risk the fortune of his daughter. I got these facts from one of Reef's clerks – a man he'd fired who was a bit sore against him. And I'd say Reef was in a pretty bad position. He knew his uncle would not hesitate to prosecute him. He went to Frensham's office, intending to make a clean breast. Mr. Main, Frensham's clerk, said that Reef telephoned an hour before he came, and as a result, Frensham ordered the clerks to go home, otherwise Main was staying late that night. It was a dull, rather gloomy evening for that time of the year. That is the only reason I can suggest for what happened afterwards. Reef must have gone and told his uncle the truth – I have an idea that Frensham, who was a passionate man, must have lost his temper and pulled a gun on him, threatened to shoot him – Frensham always kept a gun in the drawer of his desk. He then told Reef to write his confession. I don't know when the idea came to Mr. Julian – probably when he had written those lines which were found in his pocket. He must have stopped there, and by some means – on an excuse that his nerves were so bad that he couldn't hold a pen (that seems the most likely) he induced Frensham to write the confession for his signature and when Frensham had written as far as we saw, Reef shot him dead. Nobody heard it; the offices were deserted and that accounts for the ease with which he got away. When he came into the building he was wearing an overcoat and gloves. He must have had those on at the time of the murder – the coat, at any rate, for we found any number of bloodstains, as I expected we would, mostly on the right sleeve and the right breast. It was after the murder was committed that a messenger-boy came with your letter. I suppose Reef was in a bit of a panic: he told the boy to put it under the door and, scribbling a signature on the receipt, pushed it back. If I know anything about murders and murderers, he was too upset or agitated to open that letter. What he did was to tear it up and throw it in the wastepaper basket. Probably he wasn't aware that he did it till some time afterwards, when Lady Ursula told him that you had probably sent her father the money he required. That is why he came back – yes, it was he who came back – after the police and body had left. He came back the same way as he got out – through the window, and down the fire-escape. There's nothing but office buildings around and nobody saw him go. He must have discovered the bloodstains on his coat, possibly on his gloves. He may have thrown coat and gloves away – we found the coat, at any rate.'

'How ghastly!' said Tony. 'How perfectly ghastly!'

'Most murders are,' said the other drily. 'I tell you I knew this at the inquest, but hadn't got that much' – he snapped his fingers – 'evidence to support it. And then, like a gift from the Lord, came this coat. There were the bloodstains, there was the night of the murder, there was the time the coat was thrown away, and there in the pocket the beginning of a confession which he'd crumpled up and probably didn't know he'd slipped into his pocket.'

'Have you the warrant?' asked Tony.

Elk shook his head.

'No. I'm applying this afternoon – or rather, the Public Prosecutor's people are. They have all the facts.'

'Is Guelder in this?' asked Tony.

Elk pursed his lips.

'I doubt it. Yet he must know. That fellow's got more intelligence than you'd expect in a scientist. Perhaps he egged him on – he couldn't live in the same office and plan the same swindles as Julian Reef and not know, but I haven't got enough evidence to pull him in. I'd give my head to – the meanest man I've ever met. I've spoken to him a dozen times. The last time I met him he gave me a Dutch cigar – I was ill for three days!'

29

GUELDER confronted his broken employer; and from his attitude and tone a stranger, unacquainted with what had passed that morning, might have thought that it was he who had the grievance and that the young man who sat huddled in his chair, his head on his hands, was the offender.

'I forgif you everything,' Guelder was saying, loftily. 'You are stupid, you are childish, you are cur-like, you betray your friends when you could have put great faith in a great master, you assault him mit your hands – but I forgif you. You haf no heart in your body bigger as the pip of an apple! Your liver white, your soul is like water – ach!'

'Leave me alone, damn you!' came a muffled voice from behind the hands. 'Haven't you done enough?'

'I have been your frient through all adversity,' Guelder

went on oratorically. 'I protect you and I excuse you. I know you are a murderer – do I shrink from you? You discover I have been anticipating the exact operations of science, and you scream at me like a great oaf! I anticipate science, that is all. It is permissible when one has the faith. A few more months and the harmless little deception would have been unnecessary. But your great financiers and your friends, they must have immediate results – that is not the way with science, my frient!'

'Leave me alone,' growled the other.

'I will leaf you alone, but will our friend Mr. Elk leaf you alone, and the twisting man who has made so much a fortune as we have lost one? No, no my good Julian, you are panicked; you fly here and there like the little sheeps at every noise! The detective find your overcoat – ah, you must shoot the detective. You must risk everything – and in my car! And this on the eve of great possibilities!'

Julian looked up. His bloodshot eyes shot hate at the man who had encompassed his ruin.

'I suppose you know that I shall be bankrupt by the end of this week?'

Guelder broke into a fit of shrill laughter.

'Oh, so small a matter as bankruptcy! You may also be in that machine which moves so quickly to the gallows in this country. Do you realize that, my frient?'

Curiosity overcame the resentment Julian Reef felt.

'Aren't you scared yourself? I'm expecting any minute for you to be arrested.'

'For what?' demanded the Dutchman, blandly. 'For my little cheat? Oh, no! Mr. Sleser has told us he will not make himself a perfect fool for all the clever people of the City to laugh at!'

He tapped his forehead.

'I am of superior mentality.'

'Have you got any money?' interrupted Reef.

'A leetle,' said the other cautiously. 'Why?'

'I've a feeling I ought to clear out of the country.'

Guelder looked at him, speculation in his eyes.

'So!' he said at last. 'Dat is a good idea. How much money would you have?'

'A few thousands. But what's the use of asking you? You're as broke as I am, and in as bad a mess.'

'Indeed, no,' said Mr. Guelder.

He put his hand into his hip pocket and brought out a very fat bundle of notes.

'I haf taken time by the forelock. This morning I wait at the bank to cash the cheque which the generous Sleser gave me.'

'You got that money?' gasped Julian.

The man smirked.

'I can gif you two or three thousand.' He spoke very slowly, watching the effect of his words. 'Or even five thousand, if you do a small thing for me.'

'What is that?' asked the younger man suspiciously.

'If you fly from the country, what do all people say? Ah, that Rex Guelder, he is the *deus ex machina*. He is the villain of the pieces. Poor Julian, he was the catspaw! And perhaps they say "Arrest this wicked Dutchman!" I have many enemies, when I desire to have frients.'

'Well?' asked Julian impatiently, when he paused.

'There is one charming person in this town who can make things good for me. She has the ear of this twisting gentleman, possibly of the detective – I do not know. She can say "Let this poor Dutchman go in peace with his yellow diamonds and his experiments".'

'She'd never do that,' interrupted Julian. 'She loathes you! If you haven't learned that by now you're pretty dense.'

The Dutchman nodded.

'But she can be persuaded,' he said.

'Not by me.'

'Not by you, my good frient, but by me. If I could show her these wonders of my laboratory, if I could explain the latent possibilities. She has intelligence as well as beauty.'

'You mean if I could get her to come down to Greenwich to see your plant?'

Julian sneered as the Dutchman agreed that this was his suggestion.

'Do you think she'd take the slightest notice of my invitation? You're mad!'

'You can try. I do not think it would be difficult. You are a cousin, you are in a bad way, you can tell her of dreadful things that would happen to you if she does not help. She has the brains. Bring her to my house; I gif you five thousand!'

Julian vacillated. The scheme, which had seemed so utterly impracticable before, was still as fantastic – and yet . . .

Guelder's words started a new train of thought. Instinctively he knew that a net was closing around him. For two nights he had not slept; his nerves were on edge, his judgement, as he himself realized, was unstable.

'What do you think?'

Julian shook his head.

'I don't know. I'll have to consider it a little more.'

There was hope in Ursula, a faint shadow of hope. He would see her, he would plead with her, not to ensure Guelder's future but to save himself from . . . He was seized with a fit of shuddering. Happily, Guelder had gone into his little office and did not witness his exhibition of terror.

He thought of telephoning her, but decided that it would be best to take her by surprise. She might refuse to see him if she knew he was coming, but if he arrived unexpectedly he was sure of an interview. What help she could give, he did not allow himself to consider. That would be a matter to decide when he was on the way to the house.

He was very fortunate: Ursula was alone when he called, and the maid who was used to his presence in the house and had no definite orders to exclude him allowed him to walk in. At the sight of him Ursula was shocked. His face had lost its old, too healthy hue; there were deep shadows under his eyes; the hand that came out to take hers was shaking.

'Terribly sorry, Ursula,' he mumbled, 'breaking in on you like this . . . but I'm going away – the fact is, I'm really down and out.'

Though she disliked him, she could not exult. Her kindly nature offered him instead the sympathy he needed.

'It's awfully kind of you, and I've been a perfect beast, but I've never been any good from my youth up,' he said, a little bitterly. 'You're only seeing in the raw what I've hidden for so many years.'

'Are you . . .' She hesitated to use the word.

'Ruined – yes. Financially I haven't a penny. I'm overdrawn

at the bank, and if I stay in this country I shall be bankrupt.'

And then he came to the subject which had dimly loomed at the back of his mind while Guelder had been talking to him.

'That overcoat, Ursula . . . you went down to see it, didn't you?'

She nodded.

'Somebody told me that it was mine . . . I can't understand how it got to Woolwich – it was Woolwich, wasn't it? I haven't seen it for a long time – not since the night of Uncle's death.'

He saw in her eyes the fears to which she had never dared give expression, and he did not flinch.

'Naturally I don't want to get Guelder into any kind of trouble. He's a queer bird, always engaged in some mysterious piece of crookery – a fact which I've only found out recently – and on the night . . . you know the night . . . I lent Guelder my overcoat and my gloves. I never knew what became of the coat, but I'll swear I saw my gloves in his safe.'

Her relief was almost visible.

'Then Guelder was wearing it when it was thrown over the bridge?'

'Was it thrown over the bridge? Which bridge? Anyway it doesn't matter. I never thought about it again until the last few days.'

'Did Father know Guelder?' she asked.

He forced a smile.

'Know him! Why, of course! Guelder and he had one or two deals together. Something went wrong – I don't know what it was, but they had a quarrel. I think Uncle must have lent Guelder money; and I know on the day of Uncle's death he sent a note up to the office asking him to pay as he was in need of cash!'

'I had no idea—' she began, but he stopped her.

'I should hate to give evidence against this fellow, but what else can I do?'

'But is there any charge against him?' she asked, in amazement.

For a moment he was nonplussed.

'Well . . . I don't know. I should imagine he's been getting into some sort of scrape; he's been very strange lately.'

'I'm sure nobody realizes Guelder was associated with the coat. What has the coat to do with anything – that is the thing which bewilders me. Why do they attach so much importance to it?'

She had been unconsciously defending him.

'The coat? Oh, well, I suppose some crime that Guelder has committed,' said Julian vaguely. 'You never know where a fellow like that will stop. I only heard in a round-about way that the police have the coat and are using it as some sort of clue. Possibly it has to do with Uncle's murder—'

He let the word slip before he could arrest it.

'Murder?' she gasped, and gazed at him in horror. 'Murder, Julian . . . But Father shot himself!'

He did not speak, could only look at her stupidly.

'Oh!'

Now she was beginning to understand, and a wave of repulsion and loathing swept over her, as she shrank back from him.

'Then it wasn't suicide?' she asked, in a voice that was a whisper. 'He was killed . . . murdered . . . by somebody wearing your coat. And you're trying to tell me that it wasn't you, but Guelder. And it *was* you! You killed him – murdered him . . . your own flesh and blood!'

Her finger pointed accusatively. He was incapable of denial.

'Get out, before I send for the police.'

Then he found his tongue. The terror which had held him silent now augmented his fury.

'You're a pretty good pupil of The Twister. I've told you all I can without betraying a man—'

'I don't want to hear any more,' she said. She was as white as death, but with perfect command of her emotions.

'I can prove it to you,' he went on, desperately.

She pointed to the door and he went; and again luck was with him. The detectives had missed him three minutes after he left his office and now, instead of going back to the City, he turned on to the Heath, and was hardly out of sight before a big police-car swept into the road and Elk arrived, to find that his quarry had again slipped him.

30

REEF walked on blindly to Muswell Hill and then he remembered that Guelder was waiting for the result of the interview. He entered a telephone booth and called the number of a little teashop where Guelder used to be at a certain hour in the afternoon. His luck should have terrified him. Guelder answered him almost immediately and in a few agitated words told him of the police visitation.

'No, no, do not go to Greenwich, but tonight at eleven o'clock you shall be at Channey Stairs, Limehouse, and I will pick you up from the river. Keep out of sight, my frient. You remember . . . Channey Stairs.'

How could a man hide in the daytime – a red-haired man for whom the police were searching? He doubled back to Hampstead Heath, found a little clump of bushes and, crawling in, spread his raincoat and fell asleep on the half-sodden ground. When he woke he was hungry and aching from head to foot. He looked at his watch; it was dark and raining: the cool drops on his face had awakened him up from a sleep which was the most blessed adventure of the day.

It was five minutes to ten. He dragged himself to his feet with a groan, pulled on his raincoat and crossed the Heath towards Swiss Cottage. The sight of a policeman patrolling the main road sent him off at an angle and by some extraordinary combination of circumstances he found himself again outside Ursula's house.

His heart was filled with bitter rage against her; he would like to hurt her, do her some vital injury. Here was the Dutchman, a man he had tried to betray, who had stood up for him in the hour of his trouble; and she, who would have been his wife if he had only realized the value of those cursed Lulangas, had treated him like a dog, sent him out to his pursuers. He ground his teeth at the thought of his wrongs.

She hated him almost as much as she hated the Dutchman – no, she hated the Dutchman worse, she loathed him. Even the thought of Guelder brought to her a sense of physical nausea.

And then he heard a woman laugh. It was not Ursula, as a matter of truth, but the maid. But he was content that it should be Ursula, laughing at his misfortune.

And then he heard her voice distinctly in the quiet night. She was talking to somebody on the telephone, and the words carried.

'. . . No, don't be silly; I'll come by myself. I will be with you in seven minutes . . . Tony, is there any news . . . of Julian? Horrible, isn't it? And yet I can't be sorry for him.'

She couldn't be sorry for him! He grinned fiercely in the darkness. So she was going to her lover and she couldn't feel sorry for him. She was going to The Twister and she couldn't feel sorry for poor Julian Reef, hunted like a dog and starving. He shivered from head to foot with – with malignity. Every man's hand was against him – Ursula, Braid, all of them, trying to drag him into a murderer's cell . . . She hated the Dutchman, loathed him. That was a pleasant thought.

He heard her voice again, saw her car by the front door, then he stepped back behind the dripping rhododendron. He heard her start up the car, the whine of it as it moved, and then the flicker of the headlights fell on his hiding-place.

She slowed for the narrow opening of the drive gates, and as she did so he stepped out of his hiding-place. In a second he had opened the door and had dropped to the seat by her side.

In her terror she jerked round the wheel, and almost collided with a pillar-box.

'Drive on!' he hissed fiercely. 'If you scream I'll cut your heart out!'

One of his hands had gripped the wheel; it was he rather than Ursula who brought the car into the main road.

'Drive on . . . I've got to get away. I'm starving. You don't understand what that means, do you? Hunted . . . whilst you and your . . .'

She did not answer. Her heart was thumping, so that it must surely be heard above the throb of the engine. She had gone icy cold when that shape had suddenly appeared at her side; but now that she knew it was Julian, she had something tangible to fear.

'I will drive you as far as Regent's Park and no farther,' she said.

'You'll drive me just where I want you to drive me. If I tell you to drive me to Hell, that's where you will go!'

She could not misunderstand his tone, or the meaning of his tremulous rage.

'I am wanted for murder – for murdering my dear uncle. If your life stands between me and my freedom, you needn't question what will happen to you. You're not sorry for me, are you? You can get up from your dinner-table and discuss my life, my agony, as though I were a character in some play.'

His hand, which had slipped down the cushion of the car, touched something cold. It was a large iron spanner. He gripped this with a chuckle.

'And now listen to me. I've got a spanner in my hand – you know what a spanner is? It's an ugly bit of iron. It's the only weapon I've got, but it's quite good enough for me. If it gives you any satisfaction, I shot Frensham, and it didn't disturb my sleep! And I'll kill you and leave you battered out of all recognition, and that won't disturb my sleep, either. Take the next road to the left. If the policeman holds you up at the crossing, pull up some distance from him. If you try to attract his attention . . .'

'Do you realize what you're saying?' The horrified protest was forced from her. 'You've forgotten everything, Julian, every decent thing . . . or are you mad?'

'That will certainly be my defence. If I get the right kind of lawyer, I'll get off,' he sneered. 'Go right ahead now!'

They were avoiding the well-lighted streets, and that she could understand. Possibly he had no definite objective, and wanted only to get out of London.

Channey Stairs, Limehouse. He was trying hard to remember where they were. He knew Limehouse, for he had once been associated with a shipping office that had a store there. Now he remembered the 'Stairs'; a narrow passage between very high warehouse buildings, and at the end a flight of stone steps leading down into the water. A woman had once been drowned – he had seen her body brought up those steps.

'Where are we going?' she asked, after a while. And then,

as an unpleasant possibility struck her: 'I'm not leaving London. If you kill me I will not go into the country!'

He was rather balking the end. He knew the street into which the stairs led. In the days of his acquaintance, the place was a desert. One saw nobody but a patrolling policeman, but that was eight years before. A lot of changes occur ... and suppose there was a policeman, and she screamed.

He found an excuse.

'I'm going to leave the country by water. There's a boat that goes down river tonight which is picking me up, if you must know. I'm making for Limehouse – Channey Stairs. Now you know as much as I do.'

She was infinitely relieved. The terror of the unknown was replaced by the comparatively small discomfort of the known.

'I don't know Limehouse,' she said.

'You needn't know it,' was his curt reply. 'You will drive just where I tell you. When I'm in safety you may go.'

It was necessary that she should become familiar with the most critical stage of the ride.

'Naturally I'm not going to leave you with the car, ready to bolt for the nearest policeman whilst I'm waiting at the head of the steps for the boat. You'll come with me to the end of the passage and as soon as I'm picked up you can leave.'

She could only conjecture what 'going to the end of the passage' meant. It sounded rather terrifying.

'I'll wait in the car till you tell me to go. I promise you I won't move—'

'You'll do as I tell you. I'm taking no risks – haven't I taken enough?' Then he went on cunningly, 'If I could have got across London without jumping your car, I'd have done it; but I was desperate, with the police looking for me everywhere.'

That also sounded reasonable to the girl. She was calm now, her heart beating normally. She even began to take an interest in the queer part of London through which she was passing.

'This is Limehouse,' he told her.

It seemed very sordid and drab and unromantic, she thought; she had expected to find every other pedestrian abroad on that inclement night to be a Chinaman. They were distressingly European.

At his direction, she brought the car running down a street by the side of a high dock wall, and two hundred yards from the stairs he saw a policeman pass on his rounds. That was good – for it meant he would not be returning for some time. Cars were no infrequent phenomena here, for there was a line of passenger ships which had its wharf entrance on this street, and this was a sailing night.

He peered through the rain-drenched glass, recognized a building, and then the lamp-brackets that spanned the stairs.

'Stop here on the right,' he commanded.

He stepped out of the car, took a quick look up and down the street. There was nobody in sight. The thoroughfare had not changed its character; they were in a canyon of high, blind walls. Peering under the street lamp along the stair passage, he saw the glitter of water and the light of a stationary barge.

'Come on, get out,' he commanded.

That old fear was coming back to her – the flesh-creeping fear that the sight of Guelder's house had inspired.

'I can't. I swear I won't move, I'll—'

'Get out!' he ordered, and almost dragged her from the car.

He had seen nobody in the street. Two pairs of eyes had seen him from the dark recesses of a wharf gate; two prowling thieves, taking a reconnaissance of a likely store, saw the car and the man with the girl disappear into the narrow opening. 'Who's that?' growled one, and then the other said:

'The engine's running – "knock" it, Harry.'

The man passed silently down the passage. He saw the man and the girl; she was talking quickly, imploringly . . .

'They're having a row. Wait till their backs are turned.'

'I won't go any farther,' she was saying, her voice broken with fear.

Then she turned to run back; with one hand he gripped her arm, with the other stifled her scream. She struggled desperately, fighting for her life. The two night-hawks heard the struggle, and thought it was an opportune moment . . .

Neither Julian nor the girl saw or heard the whine of the

car as it was driven away. His hand gripped her throat when he saw the lights of a motor-launch: a big, white boat was circling towards the stairs. With the desperation of despair he lifted her bodily.

'If you scream I'll throw you into the water,' he whispered; but Ursula Frensham was beyond resistance.

'Guelder!'

A muffled voice answered him. The boat ground its side against the submerged steps.

'Who is dat? Some girl, my frient? No, you do not—'

'Hush, you fool! It's Ursula Frensham!'

He heard a low exclamation; a boathook scraped through an iron ring. He pushed the girl into the Dutchman's arms and followed.

'We must be careful. She will not scream? . . . There is a police patrol near by. I think we go behind that barge till they pass.'

The man hauled the big launch to the shelter afforded by an empty barge.

'The divine Ursula!'

He heard Guelder chuckle delightedly, saw him stoop over the limp form, feel the cold hands.

'If you have killed her, my frient, I shall be very angry mit you.'

'She isn't dead – she's fainted.'

'Keep your voice down,' warned the Dutchman.

He stood up by the side of the barge and peered over. A long, lean shape flashed past upstream, moving with the tide.

'It will be gone soon, then we will come out,' said Guelder in a low voice.

He heard a groan from where Ursula lay, took a big handkerchief from his pocket, folded it quickly and tied it about her mouth.

'You shall hold her hands, my Julian. Happily for us, our Freda has gone to Holland. I do not think I shall see her again.'

The boat stole out of the shadows and was soon breasting the rising tide. Kneeling by the side of Ursula, Julian made reference to the speed with which the boat was moving and the silence of the engine. Guelder expressed his agreement: he had an absurd practice of taking compliments paid to his possessions as being personal to himself.

'It is the most powerful on the river,' he said. 'Also she carries sufficient juice to take me – anywhere I wish to go. I have chosen well in this leetle boat.'

'Could you go out to sea?' asked Julian, his hopes rising.

'Even to sea. So you observe, my good fellow, how fortunate you are to have such a frient as me!'

The hands which Julian held were straining against his grasp.

'Don't move. Keep quiet. Nobody's going to hurt you. We're taking you to Guelder's place.'

He heard the muffled cry of horror and realized he had said the last thing in the world to reassure her. She struggled desperately to tear away the bandage from her mouth and in her struggle set the boat rocking.

'You must be goot, my little frient,' said Guelder's hateful voice, 'or else we must drop you in the water, and that would be tragedy of the first class!'

It was not his threat that silenced her; it was the realization that the first place Tony would look, when he found her gone, would be Guelder's house. It was no remarkable coincidence that Guelder was realizing the same patent fact.

If Tony came alone . . . but that was unlikely. The amazing Elk would be somewhere at hand, and Guelder never thought of Elk but his blood ran cold. For even the boldest and the most phlegmatic of men have their pet fears.

31

THEY were nearing Greenwich now and passing the low-lying buildings of the victualling yard; a big tramp coming upriver loomed out of the darkness – and they gave her a wide berth. She passed, an overtowering mass of metal and light and rumbling noise. They were hardly clear of her before Guelder set the nose of his boat towards the shore. They passed under the stern of two anchored barges and slowly lurched up to one of the crazy green piles of the rotting wharf before he stopped his engines. A boathook, skilfully applied, drew him without effort from one staggering timber to another, until he reached in the water-lapped building a door, the lower half of which was under water.

He manœuvred the boat till the nose pressed against the heavy portal, then he set his engine running and the little boat yawed and kicked her way forward, the door opening to admit her. They were in Guelder's boathouse and garage: in reality at high tide the far end of the garage formed a small dock.

He had left a light burning. One of his white cats crouched expectantly on a stool; and the first horror Ursula saw was those green, unwavering eyes, staring at her from the half-darkness.

Guelder helped her out of the boat, and pushed and led her to a flight of narrow stairs.

'Go before, young lady,' he commanded, and she obeyed.

At the head of the steps was a landing, and then a wider flight.

'Into the room before you – you will find a door. Wait.'

He turned a switch, and the black oaken door swung open.

'Now you must wait till I pull the blinds. For dear Julian's sake we must not be seen. Now, my young friend. Is this not a pleasant surprise?'

A click of the switch and his sitting-room was illuminated; and the cheerfulness of it, the extraordinary contrast from the scene she expected to see, took her breath away.

'It is pleasant, eh, my little home?' purred Guelder, beaming through his glasses. 'You have never seen anything so beautiful – so heart-rising?'

She was calmer now: though she hated this man she must give him credit for an elementary humanity.

'You're going to let me go, aren't you, Mr. Guelder? This is Greenwich, isn't it? I can find my way back.'

'Sure you can,' said Guelder; 'but you quite understand, my dear young lady, that our frient Mr. Julian Reef – our poor frient – is in great predicaments! I do not know what has happened, how you came, but here is der fact: you are here, a partaker of my hospitality – for a little time.'

Guelder was baffled by the girl's presence. He could hardly believe his eyes or ears when Julian had told him who his companion was. He looked wonderingly at this dishevelled man. Julian Reef seemed to have shrunk since he had seen him last. He stood by the door, rubbing one hand over the other, a furtive, suspicious look in his eyes and Mr. Guelder thought he recognized the symptoms.

'My frient, you are either drunk or hungry. If you are drunk I will give you somethings to make you sober; if you are hungry – that other door is the kitchen: but be advised – do not touch the wine. Sober was safe: drunk was caught!'

Julian turned without a word and disappeared.

'Now you shall tell me all the exciting news, sweet young lady, but you must be quick, because I think it is possible that there will be great telephoning, unless you have come of your own will. You have not? So I expected. That is unfortunate. Alas! Poor Julian must be mat!'

She told him briefly what had happened and Guelder listened with an impassive face. Her presence had multiplied any danger in which he stood. The only chance was that some time would elapse before she would be missed.

'The machine – the car; where did you leaf that?' he asked suddenly.

'At the entrance of the passage,' she told him.

He made a grimace.

'How clever of Julian: So, a policeman comes along: he sees the car and the number, he telephones; in two minutes all London knows Ursula Frensham's car is in a lonely little street by Channey Stairs. Divinely intelligent!'

173

He looked at her thoughtfully, half guessing the mood in which Julian had brought her to him, and staring and staring, and absorbing more and more of her delicate loveliness; security and caution became tertiary considerations. He had only one thought now – how he might keep inquiry at arm's length and retain this godlike girl who held his thoughts day and night, and was not a tangible reality.

He went to a deep cupboard set in the wall, took out a bottle and a glass.

'I will drink nothing,' she said determinedly. 'I want you to let me go, Mr. Guelder. Otherwise this may be a very serious matter for you. It is serious enough as it is,' she said, remembering. 'If Julian spoke the truth, you still have the gloves in your safe.'

He was so startled that he nearly dropped the bottle.

'He told you so? I have gloves mit bloodstains, yes? That is true. Are they supposed to be—? So, so, you must tell me no more. Now I understand . . . the good Julian! Such a genius! Did he speak of the coat? Ah, yes . . . and I wore the gloves too, and I killed your goot father? Was that the story? I guess well, young lady, I see by your face! Come, come, that is a news! Such strange things does Julian say. Did you tell the police, or was this said to you in the car?'

'I was told this afternoon,' she said.

He nodded.

'And of course you tolt The Twister, and The Twister told the Elks, and all the world knows.' He shrugged his shoulders. 'Such stupidity! But these gloves, they might be embarrassing. I must thank you for your kindness. And now you will drink this wine. See, I open it for you. It is the rarest Bordeaux and will give you courage. Have I poisoned it? How absurd! Did you not see me mit your own eyes bring it from the cupboard? You shall pour it out yourself, and wipe the glass, but you must drink.'

'I don't want wine,' she insisted.

'You are whiter than death. I have humanity, Lady Ursula, though you dislike me so much. I am a cunning Dutchman, full of tricks and pranks, but I have the heart!'

Reluctantly she poured out half a glassful of the wine.

'You need that, you have done so much,' said Guelder encouragingly.

She could endorse her need: she felt limp and weak; at every step up those stairs her knees had given under her. She picked up the glass and drank half its contents, knew by its velvety taste that it was, as he had said, a rare old wine.

'Now you shall sit down.'

He pushed her gently on to the deep couch near the window. She had a queer sense of lassitude, an overwhelming desire for sleep, which she struggled to master. With every second that passed, the will to struggle grew weaker. Mr. Guelder watched her sway, gently lowered her till her head was on the pillow and then put up her feet.

'What have you done?'

He turned round to meet Julian's suspicious eyes.

'I have put her to sleep. It is good to sleep.'

'Doped her?' Julian looked at the glass. 'Good lord, didn't she see you—'

Mr. Guelder smiled. He could not explain that that bottle of wine had been specially prepared, not for Ursula Frensham, but in an emergency for this uncomfortable guest of his. Uncomfortable? Dangerous – for Rex Guelder the most dangerous man in the world. He had laughed as he had guessed the story which Julian Reef had told the girl. For one second he had laboured under an overwhelming sense of fear. He had already arranged for the disposal of Julian Reef. If it were expedient – such a man might be dangerous. Down in the garage was a heavy linked chain . . . two . . . and a coil of fine wire. But only if it were expedient. He sacrificed all considerations to that factor. Julian was not content to escape: he must be guilty of that folly which is the undoing of so many criminals – a last stand in an impossible position. And he, Rex Guelder, was to be the defensive weapon. Obviously the Dutch boat for which he had arranged a tentative passage must go without its unlisted passenger; and a new way must be found for meeting a dangerous situation. Desperate diseases . . . Rex Guelder did not finish the sentence. He went into his laboratory and was busy there for ten minutes, Julian having returned to the kitchen to appease his hunger.

What must be done must be quickly done. The Dutchman

came back and looked down at the sleeping girl, feasting his eyes upon her beauty. He was standing thus when Julian returned, with a great hunk of cake in his hand.

'What are you going to do with her, Guelder?'

The Dutchman turned a smiling face.

'Dat is known to Gott and me,' he said, pleasantly.

There was an odd look in Julian's eyes. He had found his way to the wine bin in the kitchen.

'It might also be known to me, old man. I'm, so to speak, in charge of this young lady.'

Guelder did not reply.

'D'you hear?' Julian lurched towards him. He had evidently drunk very heavily, or the wine was singularly potent . . . Brandy, of course. It was foolish to leave that bottle in his way and the wine cupboard unlocked. 'I have decided that she ought to go back. I can't play that sort of trick on a girl – a relation.'

Still Guelder was silent.

'Look here, old man' – Julian came closer and slapped the Dutchman on the shoulder – 'we're both in trouble; we ought to stand together. The best thing we can do is to send her back to her Twister.' He chuckled drunkenly. 'We're the twisters, eh – the real twisters! That's the idea – send her back, and you and I will skip out.'

'Come here,' said Guelder.

He led the way into the factory. Only one light was burning, that powerful, dazzling light above the diamond machine. At the far end of the room was a door and across this was laid a steel bar; it seemed to have been put there quite recently. Guelder pointed to the door.

'If there is trouble, and I gif you warning, get through that door. On the other side is stairs that go to the river, and I keep a boat there.'

'That's an idea.' Julian regarded the door with drunken gravity.

'Soon, I think, Mr. Elk will come, and I shall have to make the explanations. It would be well if you knew your way.'

'Sure,' said Julian Reef.

He walked to the door and gripped the steel bar.

The watchful Dutchman saw him writhe terribly, heard the

whistling outflow of his breath and, reaching out his hand, turned a switch. Julian Reef dropped in a heap. He had never felt the shock that killed him.

With no effort, Guelder lifted him to his shoulder and carried the limp thing down the stairs to the boathouse. He dropped him as if he were a sack of flour into the launch, and went in search of the heavy chain. There were two. He might need two.

With a long piece of wire he bound link to link about the dead man's ankle, and then he pushed the launch towards the folding doors and jumped on board as they opened. He was in midstream in a few minutes. No sign of police patrol. He made another examination of the chained ankle and then gently slid the inanimate thing over the side of the boat. The launch lay over under the weight till its gunwale was almost level with the water . . .

Rex Guelder came back to the boathouse, as calmly and as unperturbedly as though he had gone out into the open to see what sort of a night it was.

He dragged the second chain near to the side of his little boat. It might be necessary. Then he went upstairs, stopping only to make sure that the doors were well fastened.

She was still asleep. He leaned over and brushed her cheek with his lips, then he began to take off her shoes.

32

THE police constable on traffic duty in the Commercial Road held up his hand to check a car that was crossing at right angles. The driver paid no heed to the police signal; and no doubt he would have got away, but for the fact that a big lorry blocked his crossing at the psychological moment. The policeman walked up to the car in his slow and dignified way and the driver made a mistake. He leapt out and started to run. There was, unfortunately for him, another policeman on point duty.

'Let's have a look at that licence of yours,' demanded the policeman, and then he recognized his capture. 'Get into that car, and drive me to the station. If you try any monkey tricks with me I'll beat the head off you.'

Unconsciously did he paraphrase the words that had been uttered little more than an hour before.

What the East End of London knows at ten o'clock, Scotland Yard knows a minute later. The man who sat in the instrument room at Scotland Yard heard a prosaic message, jotted down the car number and plugged in a call to the room of Inspector Elk.

'The car's been found, sir – Lady Ursula's. Picked up in the East End of London, being driven by a notorious car thief.'

'Was the lady there?' asked Elk, anxiously.

'No, sir; no report of the lady.'

The man at the wires plugged in to South London to describe a golden-headed umbrella that had been stolen from the House of Commons and was believed to be in the possession of . . .

Tony was with Elk, a singularly calm man, remembering all that he suffered.

'This bears out the story of the policeman who said he saw the car near Limehouse,' said Elk. 'You might get on to Lady Ursula's house again, and find out whether she's back.'

She had not returned, Tony learned from the tearful maid.

'Didn't expect she would,' said Elk. 'I'll know a little more about this in a few minutes.'

He waited for the inevitable call to come through from the East London police station. At last it came – from the desk sergeant. He had interrogated the prisoner, who had made a clean breast; he was a wise thief who never gave the police unnecessary trouble. He had picked up the car opposite the Channey Stairs. He had also seen a man and a woman go down the narrow entrance towards the water.

'Limehouse . . . Channey Stairs,' said Elk. 'Good!'

He tapped the hook impatiently, and Central answered him.

'Get me Thames Police Headquarters and ask them to have a launch waiting for me at Channey Stairs,' he said.

'Couldn't you phone through to Greenwich?' said the anxious Tony.

Elk shook his head.

'If she's there, you can bet that the land side of the house is so well protected that you'd have to use a battering ram to get in. He's got a wonderful back yard, that Dutchman – it stretches to the North Pole and the South. That's the way he'll bolt and I believe in trapping bolt holes.'

'Who was the man with her?'

Elk shook his head.

'The car thief didn't recognize him. He thought it was just a man and his girl quarrelling. I gather from the fact that he didn't notice any foreign accent that the man was Mr. Julian Reef. Guelder, by the way, had made arrangements for him to leave London tonight by the river. That all fits in. He was going to put him aboard the *Van Zeeman*, bound for South America. The chief steward was in it, but the purser got to hear of it and reported to the police. From the fact that the steward was told that Reef might be brought aboard drunk, it looks as if Mr. Julian didn't know very much about his trip.'

He put on a heavy raincoat and belted it about him. Then he opened a drawer of his desk and took out a very serviceable-looking Browning, slipped it into his pocket with an apology.

'I hate using guns: it looks theatrical, but I've got an idea that dear old Rex will be packing a gat. And life's very precious to me – I'm getting old. When you arrive at my age,' he went on, continuing the cheerful subject, 'you don't stop wondering how the world's going to get on without you.'

The car was waiting by the door. Near by stood two men, who without a word made themselves uncomfortable by the side of the driver.

'The joy of being a superior officer,' said Elk, 'is that you get the best seat. I may not want them at all, for these Thames policemen are pretty tough.'

In a quarter of an hour they came to Channey Stairs and

found a river police sergeant waiting for them. At the foot of the stairs was a long launch, its lights burning dimly.

'You'll have to put those lights out when we get near to the house, inspector,' said the sergeant in charge.

'Which house is this?' asked Elk, innocently.

'Guelder's, isn't it? I wasn't told, but I guessed. Anyway, we've had orders to watch Guelder's place and pick up this man Reef.'

'You'll pick up this man Reef all right,' said Elk, and he spoke prophetically.

The tide was on the turn and the launch went eastward at a respectable speed.

'I'm keeping close to the Middlesex coast,' explained the sergeant. 'I thought it might be better to cut across the river and rush the place than come on it with the stream. He might be able to spot us – there's London light on the river.'

Elk agreed mechanically. He did not know anything about the technicalities of river work.

'There's a light in the factory.' The sergeant was looking through night glasses. 'Guelder's there, anyway.'

'He's got a boat, hasn't he?'

'Yes, a pretty powerful launch. The boathouse will be the best way to get in, I think. It isn't fastened at all, as a matter of fact. About three months ago a river "rat" got in and boned three or four cans of petrol, and was nearly torn to pieces by one of Guelder's cats.'

They were opposite the house now.

'Let's go,' said Elk.

The sergeant turned the nose of the launch across the stream. Suddenly Elk felt the boat shudder.

'It's all right, I'm reversing,' explained the police officer; and then: 'Forrard there – what's that in the water?'

'Looks like a body,' said a voice.

'Claim it,' said the sergeant laconically.

A boathook shot over the side and pulled the dark bundle into the boat.

'Very sorry, Inspector, but I can't pass that. It isn't pleasant, but it's got to be done. We aren't allowed to pass a body unless we're chasing.'

Two men leaning over the bow of the boat were gripping something.

'It's a dead 'un,' said a voice. 'Can't have been in the water long.'

Elk went forward with the sergeant. Somebody held a torch over the side and, looking down over the inspector's shoulder. Tony stared horror-stricken into the sightless eyes of Julian Reef. Mr. Guelder's chain had been carelessly adjusted.

33

URSULA came gradually to her senses. She had a bad dream. She dreamed she was lying on a muddy foreshore and that out of the water appeared the slimy head of a great snake. She tried to get up and run but she could not move and she saw the spade head come closer and closer, the vile mouth open, and felt the fangs grip at her foot . . . he was pulling her into the water, pulling . . .

She looked up. Somebody was taking her shoes off. One fell on the floor with a rattle. Guelder heard her cry and turned quickly.

'It is nothing, it is nothing,' he tried to soothe her. 'You must not be alarm', my little frient. All is well. You are wit' Rex.'

The eyes that glared down at her seemed twice their normal size. They were afire with something that she had not seen in man or beast. The hands that pressed her back as she strove to rise were shaking as if the man suffered from an ague.

'It is nothing; you must be goot! Rex will look after you, my beautiful lamb!'

He knelt by her side, and putting one arm beneath her shoulder, held her lightly. She was fascinated with horror and fear, could not move or speak, could see nothing but those two round eyes quivering with mad fire and hear the murmured incoherence of his endearments. He found it difficult to speak English.

'You are better as all the womans in the world,' he said huskily. 'You are my divine dream.'

She grew sick and faint; he saw the colour leave her face, and released his hold and instantly his manner changed.

'If you look at me so I will beat you,' he said shrilly; 'and if you make sounds you will be sorry!'

He went to the table and poured out another glass of wine. 'Drink this.'

She pushed the glass away, spilling the greater part of its contents. He filled it again savagely.

'Drink!' he snarled.

'Don't move, Guelder!'

He dropped the glass with a crash and turned to face the levelled gun which Elk was holding.

'When I said "don't move", I was speaking figuratively,' said Elk. 'This is the place where you've got to start moving. Put up your hands!'

The Dutchman obeyed.

'Where's your pal?'

Guelder's face was twitching. Yet even in that tragic moment of his life he could smile.

'I show you.'

'Suppose I show *you?* He's in the police boat downstairs. How did he get there?'

And here Guelder made one of his greatest mistakes.

'In the police boat . . . he come up?'

'Sure he came up,' said Elk. 'I gather, from the wire round his leg, that you fastened something pretty heavy.'

Again Guelder shrugged.

'You wish to take me? Then perhaps I had better turn off the current in my factory. It may be dangerous for your police officers.'

'We'll look after that,' said Elk.

Again the man shrugged.

'You know best, of course.'

Then he turned his head to the sofa where Tony Braid sat, supporting the half-fainting girl.

'Ah! The Twister! You will intercede with me in the interests of science, Mynheer Braid! In this next room I have machines of the highest complications. Somebody will be hurt – I call you to witness it is not my fault.'

Elk was undecided.

'All right, walk ahead,' he said. 'If you try any funny business —'

'You will shoot me dead. That will be painful,' said the Dutchman, grinning broadly. 'I myself understand a death that is more painless.'

He went slowly down the right-hand bench.

'That I will put off,' he said and pulled over a switch. 'This door' – he pointed – 'does not open. It is what is called a blind. But this bar has a special purpose, and we will see with what extraordinary courage that Doctor Rex Guelder will face the comparatively unknown!'

Then deliberately he dropped his hands on the bar.

Elk would have gripped him, but one of the river policemen behind him grasped him by the arm and pulled him back.

'He's on a live wire. Where's that switch?'

Directly the switch was turned off the limp body of the Dutchman fell with a thud to the ground. The engineer of the boat, who had probably saved Mr. Elk from an untimely fate, went forward and examined the bar curiously.

'This operates through a transformer – he probably got seven or eight hundred volts through him.'

'Is he dead?' asked Elk, and when the engineer nodded:

'That saves a whole lot of trouble,' said Elk.

On the following pages are some other Arrow books that may be of interest:

ON THE SPOT
Edgar Wallace

Nobody ever disagreed with Tony Perelli twice.

In the Chicago gangland of the 1920s, Perelli ruled his empire unchallenged. Bootlegging, prostitution and murder were all part of his game. His ambitions were giant. And so was his ego. To get what he wanted he would use anybody, and dispose of anybody.

But in the tough Chicago no-man's-land, a king needs loyal subjects; and Perelli had to learn that loyalty can never really be bought.

85p

TO FEAR A PAINTED DEVIL
Ruth Rendell

When Edward Carnaby attempts to buy cyanide from his local chemist – supposedly to rid his house of wasps – the news rockets round the town of Linchester.

At a disastrous pary the following weekend, Patrick Selby – the richest man in the community – is unaccountably attacked by a swarm of wasps. He dies during the night. An unfortunate coincidence – or was it?

'The appearance of any novel by Ruth Rendell is a cause for celebration' *The Spectator*

80p

FROM DOON WITH DEATH
Ruth Rendell

'Britain's leading lady crime novelist' *Sunday Express*

Margaret Parsons and her husband had just moved back to the small village in which she had grown up. They lived an uneventful, anonymous life and had nothing to hide.

Why then is Margaret found horribly strangled in a wood? Why do her childhood friends deny even having known her? And who is the secret admirer who has been sending her books of poetry?

80p

SOME LIE AND SOME DIE
Ruth Rendell

For a while the pop festival at 'Sundays' went well. The sun shone, the groups played and everyone – except a few angry neighbours – seemed to enjoy themselves.

Then the weather changed. And in a nearby quarry two lovers found a body that made even Inspector Wexford's stomach lurch.

Dawn Stonor had been a local girl – back from London on a flying visit that not even her mother could explain – and the only clue that Wexford had was her strange connection with the star of the festival . . .

'One of the best crime novelists writing today' *Sunday Express*

80p

A SLEEPING LIFE

Ruth Rendell

Kingsmarkham was one of those close-knit communities where everyone knew everyone else's business; so when Rhoda Comfrey's body was found under a hedge, Chief Inspector Wexford felt sure the case would be a simple one.

But although the victim was a familiar face to the locals, there was absolutely no evidence that she existed – no address book, no driving licence – nothing but forty-two pounds and three keys. But when Wexford begins to tackle the case, it turns into a maddening labyrinth of blind alleys.

85p

CAST FOR DEATH
Margaret Yorke

'The body lay just beneath the surface of the river the hair streaming in the tide, legs splayed with the movement of the water, arms spread, the face downwards.'

That evening, Sam Irwin, noted actor, should have been appearing on stage at the Fantasy Theatre. Instead, his corpse was being hauled from the Thames.

It looked like suicide; but his friend, Patrick Grant, found that difficult to believe. He was determined to find the real reason for Irwin's death; and before long, some apparently unrelated incidents – a series of art robberies, the accidental death of a dog – appeared in a new and sinister light.

'A superior detective story, bang up-to-date.' *Evening Standard*

85p

URN BURIAL
Patrick Ruell

The unexplained death of a minor diplomat in Baghdad . . . the mysterious disappearance of a Roman skeleton from an archaeological dig . . . the suicide of a British scientist in a Californian motel. . . .

Three apparently unconnected incidents; but the secret to them all lie sin an abandoned station on Thirlsike Waste – a remote and windswept area of Cumbria where the natural and supernatural meet. . . .

'Fantastical adventure . . . in the full Michael Innes tradition.'
H. R. F. Keating, *The Times*

'A splendid story . . . grips the reader to the very last page.'
Glasgow Herald

65p

BESTSELLERS FROM ARROW

All these books are available from your bookshop or newsagent or you can order them direct. Just tick the titles you want and complete the form below.

☐	BRUACH BLEND	Lillian Beckwith	90p
☐	THE HISTORY MAN	Malcolm Bradbury	90p
☐	A RUMOUR OF WAR	Philip Caputo	£1.25
☐	2001: A SPACE ODYSSEY	Arthur C. Clarke	£1.10
☐	THE GIRL WITH THE GOLDEN HAIR	Leslie Deane	£1.60
☐	BILLION DOLLAR KILLING	Paul Erdman	95p
☐	ZULU DAWN	Cy Endfield	95p
☐	FALLING ANGEL	William Hjortsberg	95p
☐	AT ONE WITH THE SEA	Naomi James	£1.25
☐	HITLER'S SPIES	David Kahn	£2.50
☐	IN GALLANT COMPANY	Alexander Kent	85p
☐	METROPOLITAN LIFE	Fran Lebowitz	95p
☐	THE CLIMATE OF HELL	Herbert Lieberman	£1.25
☐	THE MEMOIRS OF RICHARD NIXON	Richard Nixon	£4.95
☐	THE VALHALLA EXCHANGE	Harry Patterson	80p
☐	DANGEROUS OBSESSION	Natasha Peters	£1.85
☐	STRUMPET CITY	James Plunkett	£1.75
☐	SURFACE WITH DARING	Douglas Reeman	£1.00
☐	A DEMON IN MY VIEW	Ruth Rendell	85p

Postage

Total

ARROW BOOKS, BOOKSERVICE BY POST, PO BOX 29, DOUGLAS, ISLE OF MAN, BRITISH ISLES

Please enclose a cheque or postal order made out to Arrow Books Limited for the amount due including 8p per book for postage and packing for orders within the UK and 10p for overseas orders.

Please print clearly

NAME ....

ADDRESS ....

....

Whilst every effort is made to keep prices down and to keep popular books in print, Arrow Books cannot guarantee that prices will be the same as those advertised here or that the books will be available.